Pierre M. F. Monsieur de Pagès

Travels Round the World

In the Years 1767, 1768, 1769, 1770, 1771 - Vol. 2

Pierre M. F. Monsieur de Pagès

Travels Round the World
In the Years 1767, 1768, 1769, 1770, 1771 - Vol. 2

ISBN/EAN: 9783337193300

Printed in Europe, USA, Canada, Australia, Japan

Cover: Foto ©Andreas Hilbeck / pixelio.de

More available books at **www.hansebooks.com**

TRAVELS

ROUND THE WORLD,

IN THE YEARS
1767, 1768, 1769, 1770, 1771.

BY

MONSIEUR DE PAGÉS,

CAPTAIN IN THE FRENCH NAVY, CHEVALIER OF THE
ROYAL AND MILITARY ORDER OF ST. LOUIS,
AND CORRESPONDING MEMBER OF THE
ACADEMY OF SCIENCES
AT PARIS.

TRANSLATED FROM THE FRENCH.

VOLUME THE SECOND.

———————

LONDON:

PRINTED FOR J. MURRAY, N° 32, FLEET STREET.

M.DCC.XCI.

CONTENTS.

VOLUME II.

PART II.

CHAP. I.

CHAP. II.

CHAP.

CHAP. III.

CHAP. IV.

CHAP. V.

CHAP. VI.

TRAVELS

TRAVELS

ROUND THE WORLD,

BY SEA AND LAND.

PART II.

CHAP. I.

*A Voyage from Batavia to Bombay and
Surat ; and my Abode in thofe two Cities.*

WE failed for Bombay and Surat on
the 2d of Auguft 1769, and left
Milles ifles on the ftarboard, and Honduras
with its adjacent iflands on our larboard ;
and at the approach of night found we had
cleared their feveral rocks. In the courfe of
the night we doubled Bantam, and entered
the ftreights of the Sound, and upon the return of day had left Towards-Peper confi-

derably behind us. Having ſtood ſouthward, in order to paſs between Prince's Iſland and the coaſt of Java, where we took in freſh water, we ſhaped our courſe W. and S. W. till we reached the latitude of twelve degrees; and then ſtood W.; and the wind, which had continued invariably in the S. and S. S. W. as we approached the meridian of the Maldive iſlands ſhifted into the E. and E. S. E.

Having paſſed between the iſlands of Amarante, which we could not diſtinguiſh, we immediately ſtood W. N. W. then N. W.; and having reached the latitude of ſix degrees under the meridian of the iſland Bourbon, we ſtood towards the north. The wind had blown conſtantly from the E. and E. S. E.; but here it began to die away, and continued extremely light to the ſeventh degree of northern latitude, where we had for ſeveral days calms and ſtorms alternately; after which the wind changed to the weſt.

Having been in exactly ſimilar climates previous to my arrival in the Philippine iſles, I was now, for the ſecond time, in thoſe

regions

regions at fea where the winds are regulated by the feafons; and therefore fhall take the liberty to make a few obfervations on this fubject.

In the firft place, I obferved in the ocean, as well as in the South and Indian feas, that the wind blew inceffantly from the eaft when we were near the tropics; but that it varied from the direct point towards the north or fouth, according to the precife latitude of the fhip. I have likewife obferved in all countries whatever, that when the fky is ferene the eaft or eafterly winds are much more frequent than thofe of the weft; that a north-weft wind in a northern, and fouth-weft in a fouthern latitude, are the attendants of fine weather; but the wind no fooner fhifts into the north-weft under a fouthern, or into the fouth-weft under a northern latitude, than we are with equal probability to expect rain. That with a fouth-eaft wind in a northern, and north-eaft in a fouthern latitude, we generally have rain; while the north-eaft north, and fouth-eaft fouth of the line, are the ordinary forerunners of fair weather.

I obferved

I obferved in America, the Philippine ifles, and I know the fame thing happens on the coaft of India, whither I am bound, that during the rainy feafon the wind blows conftantly from the quarter of the weft. This feafon fets in to all places between the tropics and the line, upon the fun's approaching the zenith of their refpective climates; thus the fun having croffed the equator in his progrefs northward, the rains begin to fall in all regions vifited by his vertical rays; while the correfponding parts of the globe fouth of the line enter into their dry feafon. And in the fame manner when thofe fouthern climates have their rain, the northern enjoy their fair weather. This regular courfe, however, obferved by the rain and weft winds, only extends to coafts and mainlands, or to feas, which, by reafon of their contiguity to thefe, fhare in all the accidents of their nature and fituation.

Between the tropics the eaft or trade winds blow all round the globe with no other interruption than what is occafioned

by

by vapours exhaled by the fun's rays, when he approaches the zenith of a particular climate; and then the wind fhifts its direction from eaft to weft. In the Eaft Indies thefe winds are known by the name of monfoons; in the Antilles and Ifle of France, by that of hivernage; and on the coafts of America, Africa, China, and in the interior parts of the Arabian and Perfian feas, by that of the rainy feafon. In fhort, I have obferved, that commonly in all high latitudes continued rains are accompanied with wefterly winds.

The wind being now decidedly in the weft, we ftood N. N. E. and afterwards N. E. till we came to the latitude of fourteen degrees. Here we kept the cap in the E. N. E. with the wind in the N. W.; and as we imagined we were now approaching the found, we hove the lead, and found feventy fathoms water on a fandy bottom. Having fhaped our courfe towards the eaft, we quickly difcovered land, which we found to be the mountains of Baffein, and foon came in view of Carangear and the ifle of Bombay; and as we had thirty fathoms

water

water we ſtood directly for the point of
Malabar.   Night came on, and we continued to purſue the ſame courſe till eleven,
when the water ſhallowing to twelve fathoms, with the wind at N. W. we kept
as cloſe as poſſible to the W. S. W.   We
ſtood in the ſame dangerous direction till
near five in the morning, which to ſuch as
are acquainted with the ſituation will appear a great deal too long.   Having been
carried by a rapid current greatly towards
the ſouth, at break of day we found our-
ſelves immediately under *Chaoul*.   This is a
round hill ſituated on the mainland, bear-
ing ſouth from the entrance of Bombay,
and conſequently we had fallen conſiderably
to leeward.   We attempted to recover the
advantage we had loſt by tacking; but the
wind, which blew conſtantly from the N.
W. and W. N. W. having freſhened, we
were driven about for the ſpace of two days.
Finding we had proviſions only for three
more, it was propoſed to put into a ſort of
harbour named Rajapour, ſituated in a bay of
the mainland; but beſides that it might be
particularly critical at preſent, as the period
of

of the weſt winds was drawing to a cloſe, we knew extremely little of the accommodation it afforded to ſhipping. It was then propoſed that we ſhould proceed and lay in proviſions at Goa; but as the weſt wind ſtill prevailed, it was found that if we embraced this reſolution we ſhould be under the neceſſity of croſſing the line once more, in order to get the wind for Bombay; a circumſtance which would tend greatly to protraćt the length of our voyage. In the mean time the wind ſhifted to the ſouth-weſt, and blew very freſh; when preſſing a little towards the north, in five days it became calm, and the wind ſhifting from the S. E. to the W. N. W. we again came in view of Chaoul and Carangear: and in a ſhort time ſaw the light-houſe and white rounds of Old Women Iſland. Theſe white rounds are buildings erećted with arcades, and in a circular form, for the purpoſe of beacons, and appear like ſo many large pigeon-houſes which have been lately white-waſhed. They ſtand on a low ſtrip of land, which ſtretches ſouth from the iſle of Bombay, and is known by the name of

B 4   Old

Old Women Ifland. On the ifland of Bombay are beacons of a fimilar kind; whilft one of the city churches, and the little town of Maheim, are of the fame ufe to the mariner. Maheim lies. N. W. of the ifland, and varies in its appearance by reafon of fome very tall trees, which ferve to point it out to our notice.

At the diftance of three leagues fouthweft from the ifland Bombay, we had fifteen fathoms water; and having taken a pilot on board, we failed eaftward, in order to double a reef of rocks at the point of Old Women Ifland, which ftretch in two branches fouth-eaft and fouth-weft a league into the fea. In paffing thefe rocks we kept at a league and a half's diftance from the fhore, but then veered round, putting the cap in the N. E. and afterwards in the N. N. E. being at the fame time extremely careful not to approach the coaft of Bombay nearer than feven fathoms water. We left the rocks *Sunquen* and *Droven* on our ftarboard, both of which are within the point at the light-houfe of Old Women Ifland. That of Sunquen is the outermoft, and far-

theft

theft advanced into the fea, and confequently the moft dangerous to navigation;
it lies in a direct line with the north baftion of the fort, and the houfe Maffagon.
This building is kept in repair, and white-
wafhed from time to time, for the purpofe
of a beacon; and may be diftinguifhed by
its fquare form, and its being fituated on
an eminence N. E. from the city of
Bombay. The rock Droven is near land,
and in the direction of a wood of cocoa-
trees on Old Women Ifland, and a tall
cocoa-trunk N. W. from the fort. This
wood of cocoa-trees fhould be made to
open a little in the weft, I mean fhift their
pofition a little weft of the above-mentioned
cocoa-trunk, which is kept ftanding for
this purpofe alone. It was impoffible for
us to difcover this rock without failing
too near the fhore; and therefore fteering N.
and N. and a quarter N. E. we left a little
ifland named Crofs on our left, at a very
fmall diftance. As foon as we got into
the road, we coafted the ifland Bombay at
the diftance of a ftone's caft from the beach.
I have only one word more, in the way of
caution

caution to the pilot in approaching this shore, and that is, to be on his guard against another rock, called Middle-Ground, which is situated E. and a quarter S. E. at the distance of a short league from the church of Bombay. The ships come to anchor between this rock and the shore, close to the town, which they may approach within a speaking distance in perfect safety.

Old Women Island is separated from the isle of Bombay only by a reef of rocks, which are never wholly under water, except during the high tides; and even then, though the island is on a level with the surface of the water, still it is extremely difficult of access, from the dangerous rocks with which it is surrounded. The communication between Old Women Island and Bombay lies entirely under the eye of a battery. We now began to observe the glacis of the city, whose walls border on the sea, and at the same time a couple of batteries placed in the front of the glacis. The top of the ditch, besides being under a bastion, is secured by a work more particularly

particularly intended for its defence. The cannon of this baftion and its curtine, as well as thofe of the oppofite baftion, with a double battery, by which the former are flanked, are all meant for the protection of the bay.

There is a creek occafionally ufed as a harbour, on the confines of which ftand an arfenal, dry docks, and houfes for the accommodation of the company's fervants. The city wall, interrupted by the principal harbour, re-appears at this little creek, and extends all the way to a fort which was erected by the Portuguefe. This city, though well fortified on the fide of the fea, is in but an indifferent ftate of defence towards the land, being only inclofed by a plain wall mounted with a number of pitiful little baftions. It is furrounded however by a very deep ditch, and a glacis, which is kept in excellent repair, befides that feveral of the gates have the additional advantage of half-moons. There is in its vicinity an eminence named Hongary, which appears to me to be of the greateft importance to the fecurity of Bombay.

7 The

The city of Bombay, though confiderably populous, and containing a number of hand-fome houfes, is for the greateft part ill built and very irregular.   The principal fuburbs are Hongary and Palmeyra, the laft of which is crouded with Indians, and by far the moft pleafant.

The ifland is in general extremely narrow, not exceeding in fome places half a league; but fpreads out to a confiderable extent in the quarter of Maheim.   It is extremely fteep, furrounded with rocks confifting of gravel combined with a little earth, and is every where difficult of accefs, not except-ing even the bay, particularly at low water. The inland country, though not very high, is for the moft part of an uneven and rug-ged furface.   But the excellent accommoda-tion it affords to fhipping rendering it the firft harbour on the mainland of India, and not the advantages of its foil, was the great inducement to fettle on this ifland.   It is a ftrong hold of infinite importance to the Englifh, and indeed may be con-fidered as the bafis of that extenfive do-minion

minion they have found means to eftablifh in this part of the world.

The fterility of its foil renders living at Bombay difficult and expenfive; the Englifh, however, are fupplied in provifions by the Marrattas of Salfet, Baffein, and other parts of the mainland. The late extenfion of the Englifh boundaries in thofe regions has greatly enhanced the value, as well as added to the fecurity, of this fettlement.

The veffel on board of which I took my paffage from Batavia having now accomplifhed her bufinefs at this port, I refolved to be her paffenger to Surat; and accordingly we weighed, and got under fail the 25th of September. The wind blowing almoft fair into the mouth of the harbour, we were obliged to tack; and on this occafion two reefs of rocks, which extend confiderably into the fea, and which are named Carangear's Feet, and the Rock of Chaoul, from certain hills in their vicinity, gave us much uneafinefs. Chaoul is a large high hill, nearly of a circular form, and is fituated on the mainland fouth from

† Bombay.

Bombay. Carangear is likewife a pretty high hill, ftanding on a little ifland nearer the mainland than that of Bombay. It rifes in the form of two pyramidal fections, which prefent the eliptic curve, and are diftinguifhed from each other by the Great and Little Carangear.

Having doubled the rocky points of Old Women Ifland, we fhaped a N. N. W. courfe, in twelve fathoms water. 'Here the land breeze, which came from the S. E. was very inconfiderable, while that from the N. W. and confequently againft us, was much more powerful. But in fhort, after being carried greatly towards the fouth, and much retarded by currents, tides, and winds, we came, on the eighth day, in view of Cape St. John, which forms the entrance to the gulph of Cambaia. The fituation of this gulph may be afcertained by the peak of St. John, which is only a little to the fouth of it, and which fprings from a deficiency in the mountain in the fhape of a needle. Next day we doubled the cape, but at the diftance of four leagues, in order to avoid the rocks in its vicinity.

We

We kept in foundings from fifteen to eighteen fathoms water, carefully avoiding thofe of twelve on the fide of the main, as they border on a reef of dangerous rocks, which ftretch up the middle of the gulph. We fteered acrofs a curvature, formed by a fweep of the Marratta and Damum coafts, and on the 6th of September we faw the fhipping which lay at anchor in the harbour of Surat. Next day we entered the road; and came to our moorings in ten fathoms water, on a bottom of clay. This is a very large and beautiful road, but expofed to all winds, and at too great a diftance from land.

In the prefent feafon, the fea runs with much lefs violence than either at Bombay or in the gulph; but during the rainy months, befides that the adjacent grounds are completely overflowed, it is impoffible to lie at anchor in the road, on account of a ftrong current, the inundations of the river, and the very high winds that fet in from the ocean. The moft convenient ftation for fhipping is at a village fituated on the right fide, and about the diftance of a league from

from the point of the firft bank of the river.
The city of Surat ftands on the left, about
five leagues from the mouth of the river.
In the dry feafon it is only navigable fo
high up to fmall veffels of three hundred
tons; but in the rainy months the largeft
fhips of the road fail up and winter at
Surat. As foon as we dropped anchor I
fet out for the capital; and the caftle, which
ftands on the border of the river, and within
the bounds of the city, was the firft object
of my attention, a piece of fortification,
which though irregular, and executed· in a
ftyle very different from the European tafte,
is not without merit. It confifts in a number of femicircular towers, mutually flanking
each other, and commanding the city and
river. The adjacent grounds to a confiderable extent are free from all incumbrances; but the main building, originally
well conftructed, is very old, and in want of
many repairs, efpecially on the fide of the
river. The Britifh and Moorifh flags are
equally difplayed from a baftion of the
caftle; but, though the Englifh troops have
only poffeffion of certain gates and a fingle
baftion,

baftion, all real authority both in town and country is known to refide in them. The remaining gates are occupied by the forces of the Nabob, who however, like all other Indian princes in their alliance, is allowed the exercife of his prerogatives only in matters of little moment.

Two gates in the exterior wall (for properly Surat confifts of two cities, the one erected in the bofom of the other) are in the hands of the Marrattas of Guzurat, who receive a kind of tribute from the inhabitants when they are in condition to exact it by force.

The prodigious extent of this city, its vaft population, the immenfe wealth of fome, and the affluent or eafy condition of the people in general, the numerous carriages, a moft extenfive commerce, the many beautiful houfes in the Moorifh tafte, the cheapnefs and abundance of all the neceffaries of life; every object, in fhort, within the walls of Surat, tends to imprefs the mind of a ftranger with ideas of its amazing refources and importance.

During my fhort refidence here, I faw

Vol. II.   C   the

the Nabob make his appearance in public. His highnefs was efcorted by three thoufand regular troops, befides an equal number of men on foot, on horfeback, or in palanquins ; a proceffion well calculated to give fome idea of Afiatic pomp and magnificence. In his train was a band of mufic, remarkable only for its noife, a number of camels, and four elephants richly caparifoned.

But what I admired moft is the induftrious character of both male and female among the Gentoo Indians. Befides a few of the Banians, who attach themfelves to the purfuits of commerce, the Gentoos of the inferior cafts perform all the drudgery and fevere labour of the country. Some of thefe cafts, I underftand, are believers in the ancient Metempfychofis.

There is here a race of people named Perfians, or Guebres, who ftill retain fome remains of the law of Zoroafter, and who adore the Divinity under the fymbol of fire. They are eminently diftinguifhed by their works of charity, having erected hofpitals for the accommodation of the fick and
difeafed,

difeafed, as well as for feeding the deftitute
of the inferior animals.

Many things are related of the Yoguis, or
penitential Gentoos, which may feem fomewhat incredible. There are fome among
them, I was affured, who pafs their lives with
one arm ftretched in the air; others, without
ever treading the ground, make the tour of
a kingdom by crawling on their bellies;
while a third fort remain pinned to the
fpot whereon they have been accidentally
placed, and, were no charitably difpofed perfon to interpofe and draw them afide, rather than quit their poft they would fuffer
themfelves to be crufhed to death by any
object that happened to be paffing on the
road.

One day I met with one of thofe Yoguis
preaching near a pagoda, on the border of a
lake, and at the fame time doing penance,
but of a nature which a fenfe of decency forbids me to mention. The whim of
the moment induced him to follow me
during my excurfion, nor was it by any
means in my power to get rid of him
before we returned to the border of the

C 2

lake

lake where I had found him. The penitential Gentoo is held in high veneration among the people, who refuse him nothing he afks, and permit him to take, at his diſcretion, whatever he has occaſion for. In the houſe of a banian, whom I was going to wait upon, when I was followed by this Yoguis, he ſeized and carried off ſeveral little articles, without apparently giving the ſmalleſt offence.

All the inhabitants of the firſt diſtinction in Surat, and at leaſt one half of thoſe of inferior condition, are followers of Mahomet; next to them in number are the Gentoos; then the Perſians; while the Jews and Chriſtians, the laſt of whom do not exceed five hundred perſons, make the ſmalleſt claſs.

CHAP.

CHAP. II.

*A Tour from Surat to the Island of Salset ; my
Return through the Country of the Mar-
rattas, by the Province of Guzurat and
Bassan ; my Abode in various Places.*

BEING extremely defirous to obtain
fome knowledge of the Marratta
tribes, I got myfelf dreffed in the fafhion of
that country; and, having obtained a guide
from the fame nation, fix days after my
arrival I departed from Surat. In my progrefs through the country, I paffed villages at regular ftages of four leagues, and
fometimes at a fhorter diftance. In their
vicinity are crops of Indian corn, fome rice,
vegetables, a fpecies of grain from which
they are ufed to extract oil, and another,
from the ftalks of which they acquire
materials for cordage. This country is
much interfected with rivers, which however are very inconfiderable, except in the
rainy feafon. After a journey of ten leagues

C 3   I came

I came to a fmall town called Naufary, but containing a very confiderable cotton manufactory.   It has a fort, which belongs to the Marrattas, and is furrounded with pagodas, gardens, and beautiful flower-plots. The unufual familiarity, common in this country, among all the different tribes of animals, which fport before us with the moft carelefs indifference, is not a little furprifing to a ftranger.   The birds of the air, undifmayed by our approach, perch upon the trees and fwarm among the branches, as if they conceived man to be of a nature equally quiet and inoffenfive with themfelves; while the monkey and fquirrel climb the wall, gambol on the houfe-top, and leap with confidence and alacrity from one bough to another over our heads.   Even the more formidable quadrupedes feem to have loft their natural ferocity in the fame harmlefs difpofitions; and hence the apprehenfions commonly occafioned by the proximity of fuch neighbours, no longer difquiet the minds of the natives.   Happy effect of thofe mild and innocent manners,

whence

whence have arisen peace and protection
to all the inferior animals!

The people are divided into different
casts, the lowest of which are permitted by
their rules to eat flesh on particular occa-
sions; those of an intermediate order eat
fish, fruit, and vegetables only; while the
Banian and Bramin, who belong to the
highest cast, live on nothing but the produce of the soil, in which however milk and
butter are included. Finding myself much
fatigued, upon my arrival at Naufary, by my
late journey on foot, I hired an ox, the
only animal used for the saddle in this country and continued my travels to Gondivy.
Having sat down to dine, I was a good deal
surprised to observe leaves spread on the
table instead of plates, which, upon finish-
ing my meal, I was obliged to throw away
with my own hands. I was at the same
time presented with a leaf-goblet, which,
after being used, was disposed of in like manner. It is said that a strict Gentoo would rather submit to martyrdom than defile the purity of his person, by coming in contact with
that part of the cup which has been at the

C 4   mouth

mouth of a man of a different caſt. The Moor,
the Gentoo, the Perſian, and Chriſtian, all obſerve the ſame extreme delicacy in regard to
each other. In the town of Gondivy, a very
conſiderable proportion of the inhabitants
are Perſians, and of the ſame ſect with thoſe
I ſaw at Surat. The Perſians, or Guebres as they are ſometimes called, are a
people deſcended from the ancient inhabitants of Perſia, who, upon being expatriat-
ed by their conqueror on account of their
religion, migrated hither, and their poſte-
rity are now ſcattered all over this country.

Having proceeded eight leagues further,
in a country fit only for paſture, and in
many places in the moſt deſolate ſtate, I
arrived at Gondivy in Pardy, a ſmall town,
which forms the domains of a little ſovereign prince. Next day I reached De-
mum or Damum ; but, as I had no inclination to ſee the governor, whom I ought
to have waited upon, I went on without
ſtopping, and came to ſleep a quarter of
a league diſtance, in a little town compoſed
of Gentoos and a few Chriſtians. They
are

are fubjects of the Portuguefe, who poffefs a fmall territory, and about four leagues
of this coaft, comprehending five or fix
villages, on a dry and inhofpitable foil.
This people are fo poor and neceffitous,
that I have feen Chriftians themfelves obliged, for fubfiftence, to enter as labourers
into the fervice of the Marrattas; a ftate
of indigence, however, which has hitherto
been unable either to fubdue their arrogance or ftimulate their induftry. Thus far
on my way from Surat, I had not met with
a fingle Chriftian; here, however, I difcovered my hoft to be a man of the fame religious perfuafion with myfelf. In the courfe
of the next day, I paffed very handfome
villages belonging to the Marrattas of Nar-
guoil and Barauly; and the day following,
after being a week upon the road, I arrived
at the village of Danou, the minifter of
which, an Indian Portuguefe, I made it my
bufinefs to wait upon.

This diftrict of Damum was formerly
conquered and poffeffed by the Portuguefe,
and only paffed within thefe thirty years
under the dominion of the Marrattas; who,

granting

granting toleration to all religious sects, the Christians have become frequent in every part of the country. In this village is a church, a pastor, and a very considerable body of Christians. I was invited to a marriage in the neighbourhood, at which the Marrattas, and even the Bramins, who were led by curiosity to attend this festival, some at the ceremony of the church, others at the subsequent diversions, conducted themselves with such decency of behaviour, as in similar situations we but rarely meet with among Christians, particularly where they find themselves lords of the country. Religious processions, the ceremony of burial, the use of the cross on the highways, and in general all the rites of Christian worship, are exercised here with equal freedom as in the kingdom of France.

The appearance of the Marrattas, of both sexes, particularly that of the women, confirms me in the opinion I early formed of their active and industrious dispositions. There are however among the natives some who affect to be Portuguese, but who

in

in fact are Gentoo Chriftians, and feem to
have attached themfelves to the religion
and fociety of the Portuguefe from no
other motive than that of having it more
eafily in their power to pafs their lives in vanity and idlenefs ; an abufe, however, probably proceeding from that miferable example of the Chriftian life, which the convicts
of the parent country, whom it has been
ufual to tranfport hither for their crimes,
offer to the imitation of the natives. The
Gentoos are fociable, humane, and hofpitable ; and, during my refidence in their
country, I never had occafion to obferve a
fingle inftance of violence or difpute. They
rear numerous herds of cattle ; but fuch is
their veneration for thefe animals, on account of their ufeful and patient fervices to
man, that to kill or even maim one of them
is deemed a capital offence.

Among their innumerable pagodas I faw
various kinds of beafts, trees, and even
ftones. The moft grotefque and extrava-
gant of thefe figures are emblematical re-
prefentations of the Divinity; while their
other idols, of every denomination, are of

inferior

inferior order, and only intitled to their ado-
ration as they are the reprefentatives and mo-
nitors of particular favours they have received,
from time to time, from the beneficence of
the Deity. Like the Perfians and Muffulmen,
they make frequent ufe of water for the
purification of their bodies; but of fuch
only as is contained in particular lakes;
one of them I faw between Baffan and
Agaffan, on the borders of which ftand
a number of very fine pagodas. I was
affured by a Bramin, with whom I had
the pleafure to make an acquaintance in
my peregrinations through this country,
that he worfhipped one God only; who, after having cleared the world of giants and
malefactors, had afcended into heaven. I
am far from being inclined to charge this
people with idolatry in the vulgar and li-
teral fenfe of that word; indeed in ftrict
language I can fcarce fuppofe there is one
real idolater on the face of the earth; for,
although the Divine effence is often adored
under fome material form by which he is
meant to be reprefented, ftill I am perfuaded there is no race of men, how barba-

rous

rous foever, who worſhip an idol on its own account, diſtinctly from its great original. I once entered into converſation with a Bramin, in a Chriſtian church, while the prieſt was adminiſtering the ſacrament of baptiſm to an infant, and was at pains to explain to him the duties and obligations which I conceived to be implied in that rite. Having liſtened with attention, he ſeemed much pleaſed with the lame account I was able to give of them, and concluded his reply by obſerving, that the great objects of both our religions appeared to him to be the ſame.

During the ſhort time I paſſed in this village, a little fleet of their ſhips of war, about the ſize of our tartan, entered the river. They are called *Galvettes*, and made to carry four and ſometimes ſix cannon. Their chief employment is to ſcour the coaſts of a race of pirates named *Chamchas*, who iſſue from the bottom of the gulph of Guzurat, and commit depredations upon ſuch trading veſſels as they happen to ſurpriſe in thoſe ſeas.

On the 12th of November, having re-
ſumed

fumed my journey, I paffed Trapore, a city
of fome extent, populous, and defended by
a fort. My next ftage was Mahim, a large
town, inhabited chiefly by Bramins; and the
day following I came to Agaffan, where I
lived with a Frenchman, who had the command of thirty Europeans, in the fervice of
a Rajah or Marratta prince, at Barauda, in
the province of Guzurat. The Rajah of
this province refides at *Puna* or Poney, a
large city, fituated in the interior parts of
the country, and is one of the moft powerful of thofe princes.

Agaffan ftands at the diftance of five
leagues from another confiderable town,
named Baffan, which having the advantages
of a good road and excellent river, fits out
fhips for the purpofe of trading along the
coaft of Arabia. The fea-coaft is very
ftrongly fortified, while the country from
Trapore is extremely populous, and enli-
vened with frequent and beautiful gardens.
Befides plenty of herbs and vegetables, the
inhabitants cultivate the fugar-cane, cocoa,
and fig-trees. And in the whole way from
Baffan to Agaffan, the traveller fcarce meets
                                    with

with a fingle rood of wafte or fallow-
ground. The rich verdure, however, and
vegetation of their gardens are, in a great
degree, owing to the common ufe of wheel-
wells, which are made to water the foil, by
means of buffaloes ; but in the more central diftricts, and even along the coaft from
Tropore, the foil is in general extremely
dry during the fix months of fair weather.
In the rainy feafon, on the contrary, it is
wholly under water ; and then there fprings
up an amazing quantity of grafs, which,
as the ground is either too moift or too
dry to give birth to a fingle fhrub, gives
the face of the country the appearance of
one continued meadow. The moft common tree, in the environs of Surat, is the
wild date, as is a fpecies of wild palm in the
more inland country. The chief advantage the natives derive from thefe trees
confifts in their fap, which they are accuftomed either to drink in its natural ftate, or
to manufacture into a kind of brandy. The
wood and leaves are likewife of ufe in
the conftruction of their houfes. Indian
corn is the prevailing crop in the quarter
of

of Surat, and rice in the parts which are
fituated more to the fouth. The natives
difcover fkill as well as induftry in the
cultivation of their farms. As foon as the
annual floods have withdrawn, the grafs,
which has in that interval grown up, having been collected in heaps, is burned, and
the afhes are employed as manure for the
purpofe of enriching their rice fields. The
crops of rice and corn are raifed by very
different methods. The Indian farmer,
having fowed his rice in a place well prepared and manured for the purpofe, at a
certain period of its growth tranfplants it
into a new field, where it remains till it
comes to maturity, and is cut down.

The extreme fcarcity of water, which
prevails here conftantly for the fpace of fix
months in the year, ferves to exercife the
humanity and beneficence of certain pious
and well-difpofed perfons. Hence thofe
deep wells, which have been dug and conftructed at a great expence, with the convenience of ftairs reaching to the edge of
the water; while a fund is allotted for the
purpofes of affording them occafional repairs,

pairs, of maintaining a number of water-
men, and of furnifhing fuch utenfils as are
neceffary for drawing water and giving
drink to the cattle.

In other places it has been found expedient to conftruct large and capacious ponds,
which ferve to collect water during the
rains, and to preferve it for public ufe in the
courfe of the dry feafon. Such are the dimenfions of many of thofe vaft refervoirs,
that the water is neither unwholefome nor
unpalatable; and is in a particular manner
the refource of the natives who live at a
diftance from rivers.

The moft common animals in this
country are tigers, monkies, and wild dogs,
which are fmaller in fize than thofe of
America. Of the feathered tribes, I faw
the turtle-dove, fome peacocks, numbers of
parroquets, one or two fpecies of fmall birds,
and crows in vaft flocks, and fo tame that
they ufed to attack the difhes upon the table.
The other native animals of eaftern countries defcend but feldom from the mountains, preferring, under the fhelter of their

Vol. II.   D   woods,

woods, a cooler and freer air than is to be found in the plain.

The houfes in the country are but fimple cottages, in fome places conftructed with bamboo, in others with the palm-tree, and thatched with leaves or hay. The wall confifts of wattled work of ofiers and bull-rufhes plaiftered over with mud. The town houfes, however, are extremely different, many of which have a noble effect. In general they are only of two ftories; but each floor confifts, if I may ufe the expreffion, of three amphitheatrical gra-dations, upon the higheft of which, and . in the oppofite corners, are two apart-ments, intended to contain the moft valu-able family effects. The front of the build-ing is fupported on the infide with a certain number of pillars, and open to the day; whilft the outer wall is furrounded by a kind of gallery, which embraces the other three fides of the houfe. The area of the firft gradation is laid with fine tapeftry, and here the family is accuftomed to receive and entertain their friends; it fupports likewife a large bafon, which is filled with

water

water by means of a wheel-well, the machinery of which is erected in the firſt ſtory. The buffalo employed to work the machine turns the pivot, which is over his head, in his progreſs round the circumference of the well. The floor is paved with a certain compoſition, conſiſting of a ſoft ſtone pounded and mixed with a ſpecies of plaiſter made of oil and the whites of eggs. This cement, when properly prepared, becoming extremely ſolid and compact, acquires the appearance of a ſmooth ſtone of a fine varniſh, and has a more beautiful effect than that of our beſt inlaid floors. On the top of the building is a flat roof or terrace coated with the ſame cement, which they name *algamaſſe*.

The dreſs of the women is compoſed of a very long piece of painted callicoe, one half of which, after paſſing ſeveral times round the waiſt, is folded back and faſtened behind; the other half is thrown over the head, and falling down before, covers the arms and boſom, and is attached in folds to the girdle. In this manner one ſimple garment embraces the whole body, and even

ſerves

ferves for a veil to the face. In the country,
however, they frequently gather together
what covers the head, and let it fall upon
the fhoulders, leaving the neck and bofom
almoft compleatly expofed, and on thefe occafions, as it confifts of a very fine kind of
cloth, it affumes the air of a fafh; but
when at other times they choofe to fold
up the lower part of the robe, paffing the
end of it between the legs, it acquires the
appearance of drawers, which defcend to
the middle of the thigh.

In town the men are ufually dreffed in a
long white robe, which has the appearance
of a jacket fewed to a kind of petticoat;
but in the country they wear two long
broad pieces of cloth, the one round their
loins, the other over their fhoulders, or
perhaps only a fort of band paffed between
their thighs.

Rings feem to be a peculiar object of
female ambition in every rank and condition of life, and are ufed to adorn the
toes as well as the fingers. A bracelet of
glafs tied round the wrift, and of filver
round the ankle, are extremely common;
and

and befides the ordinary ornaments of the ear, many of them wear a nofe-jewel, or ring paffed through the feparation of the noftrils. On the forehead is fometimes a ftar punctured in the flefh; and the lower eye-lafhes are often painted black, in order to enhance the brilliancy of the pupil.

The Gentoos feldom inter, but more frequently burn the bodies of their dead; a rite ufually performed on the border of a river, over which they afterwards fcatter the afhes of the deceafed. A widow commonly mourns a year for the lofs of her hufband, and in this period devotes the firft moments after fhe awakes in the morning to tears and lamentations.

There are ftill ladies, particularly in the higher cafts, who infift upon their privilege of burning upon the funeral piles of their hufbands; but on fuch occafions it is the bufinefs of the affiftants to fuffocate the unhappy victim, by pouring pails of oil over her face, before fhe has been attacked by the flames. This religious attachment of the wife to the remains of her hufband is neverthelefs greatly on the decline.

On

On the 6th of December I proceeded by Baſſan to the iſland Salſet, which is ſeparated from the mainland by a branch of the ſea, in ſome places extremely narrow, and is only two leagues in breadth where I paſſed it.   It is detached from the iſland of Bombay by another little arm of the ſea, which the Engliſh deſerters eaſily ſwim acroſs in their way to the Marratta forts of Varſova and Bandora.   Salſet is eight leagues in breadth ; and being covered with the mango, and other fruit-trees, which bear abundance of little fragrant bloſſoms, is much more pleaſant than the mainland ; but its gardens are few, and the ſoil not fertile.

I dwelt nearly in the centre of the iſland, at a town named Pary, and only at a ſhort diſtance from Malart.   This laſt place is the reſidence of an Avaldor, deputy to the ſoubadar or governor of the province, who lives in a kind of fortreſs, called Tana, about five leagues diſtant.   Pary is in the vicinity of a fountain and two reſervoirs, garniſhed with magnificent trees, and is placed in a moſt agreeable and rural ſituation,

tion. Here I made acquaintance with feveral Bramins, from whom I received in many inftances much kindnefs and civility.

The Marratta provinces are under the fupreme authority of Puna, but are adminiftered by governors, who delegate their power to commandants within their refpective jurifdictions. It is the duty of the Avaldor or commandant to collect the taxes, and in general to execute the orders of the foubadar, by means, if neceffary, of an armed force confifting of a body of feapoys.

Property in land is not transferable as in Europe, but remains vefted exclufively in the fovereign, who farms it to the peafantry, and receives a rent in kind, which has continued fixed from time immemorial at a certain proportion of the crop. This rent paid to the ftate is extremely moderate; and in order to encourage the induftry of the colomby, or farmer, who forms a caft by himfelf, he is allowed certain chiefs, whofe bufinefs it is to protect him in all the rights of his order. Other public burdens are very inconfiderable, not exceeding the annual fum

of

of five livres a family. As a particular encouragement to gardening, whatever portion of ground the farmer choofes to employ in this manner he poffeffes rent-free for the fpace of ten years, at the expiration of which period he pays to the *circar,* that is government, a third part of the produce. The foubadar is a kind of farmer general, who becomes bound to the fovereign in a certain fum for all the taxes of the province, and then collects them from the peafantry in the beft manner he can. The farmer, however, is in little danger of being oppreffed, on account of the power and confequence of his chief, who is appointed by the ftate exprefsly for his protection. The public repairs of the province of every defcription, and the purveyance of the governor's houfehold, are fervices performed by the people of whatever religion or fex; for which, however, they receive a fmall gratuity.

Towards the end of January 1770, after making a confiderable ftay on this ifland, having learned that a fhip belonging to the French Eaft India company, called

The

The Indian, anchored at Surat, I was defirous to embrace this opportunity of writing to my friends in Europe. Departing,
therefore, from Salfet, I arrived in five days
at Danou, whence it is eafy to have letters
conveyed to the city of Surat; and as I
returned by Baffan, I had a fecond opportunity of admiring the fimple but civilized
and well-regulated manners of the natives.
In the genius of the inhabitants, however,
there are certain fhades of difference, chiefly
arifing from the variety of religious opinions tolerated and exercifed in the country. The Portuguefe, as I have already
obferved, are vain and indolent; the Mahometans, with all their fimplicity, are
haughty, and ever prone to conceive themfelves of a condition fuperior to other men ;
the Perfians, or *Guebres* as they are fometimes called, are an active and induftrious
people; while the Gentoos, and above all
the Bramins, are of unaffected fimple
manners, gentle, regular, and temperate in
the whole conduct of their lives. Although
all public offices center in the caft of the
Bramins, they are peculiarly affable and
conde-

condefcending; infomuch that I am fatisfied they are ftrangers to a phrafe fufficiently intelligible in the nations of Europe,
I mean *infolence of office*. The different
chambers of adminiftration, as well as
the courts of juftice, are open to the
infpection of the public; while thofe who
prefide over them are equally acceffible to
the pooreft peafant with men of the firft
diftinction.   Here the foubadar exercifes
all the functions of his office in ·perfon;
and I have feen him, on different occafions,
with no other robe than a linen covering
tied round his loins, feated with his legs
acrofs on a carpet, writing on his knees,
or liftening with great attention and humanity to the various fuits before him.   It
was difficult for me to affociate this aftonifhing fimplicity and benignity of character
with the authority and importance of a fovereign; or to connect in my mind the notion of an extenfive population, a highly
cultivated country, a numerous army, forts,
garrifons, circumftances all expreffive of a
large, civilized, and opulent kingdom, with
the

the innocent and inoffenfive adminiftration
of its rulers.

Upon my firft arrival at Salfet, the
deputy foubadar, after receiving me in the
beft manner, took occafion to obferve, that
as Europeans were men of a fiery and tur-
bulent character, he would be glad to be
informed who was to become furety for
my good behaviour while I remained in the
country. I anfwered, that in ordinary
cafes, the maxims of our police required no
other pledge of a man's obedience to the
laws, than his perfon and property. He
replied, that a ferocity of mind, peculiar
to Europeans, and wholly incompatible with the mild genius of the natives,
had obliged him to difmifs fome of them
from the country; but that to have recourfe to their perfons or property was a
procefs which muft be attended with too
much trouble and inconvenience. The
fact was, that a few determined Europeans,
in a late inftance, had put a large body of
fepoys to flight, and, elated by their fuccefs,
proceeded to take poffeffion of feveral villages. Europeans are apt to entertain the

8   falfe

falfe idea, that they never can do enough
in fupport of their national character for
bravery, and hence are fometimes betrayed
into the moft unwarrantable exceffes;—
while, ftrange as it may feem, were thefe
ferocious Europeans, fo fuperior to the
Moors of India, to be placed in any province of the Ottoman empire, by fome un-
accountable fatality we fhould prefently find
them the inferiors of the fame people, I
mean the Moors of Turky.

This gentle difpofition of the natives of
India is probably owing in a great degree to
temperance, and a total abftinence from animal
food. The common ufe of this diet, in the
bulk of other nations in the world, has I
believe exalted the natural tone of their
paffions; and I can account upon no other
principle for the ftrong harfh features of Muffulmen and Chriftians, compared with the
fmall trait, and placid afpect of the Gentoo.
Whoever has not had an opportunity of
making this comparifon, may find it difficult to underftand what is meant by this
relative coarfenefs of feature; but in the
part of India where I now refide it would
be eafy to illuftrate it in many inftances,

by

by only placing together two natives of the fame province.

The manner of life led by a Bramin may, I have no doubt, contribute likewife to the fame effect. His refidence in the neighbourhood, but feldom within the walls, of a great town, is placed in the midft of extenfive gardens; and this, by the bye, is the true reafon why the fea-coaft all the way from Trapore is bordered with garden-ground; and hence too the very populous ftate of that part of the country; whilft at Baffan, a large and well-fortified city, I met only with military men, whofe families were in the country. Now this retired and half folitary life of the Bramin deprives him of none of the innocent plea-fures of fociety; but it exempts him from a thoufand difagreeable and painful in-cidents, unavoidable to thofe who live within the gates of a city. The perpetual verdure of his retreat; the prefence of his trees and his flocks; an intire freedom from the irkfome ceremony infeparable from great focieties, whereby a man often finds himfelf hampered even in his own family; thefe,

thefe, in fine, and other circumftances, all tending to lead man back to his firft and natural ftate, may account for that benign temper of mind, as well as for thofe peculiarities of feature, obfervable in the Bramin.

Their laws are the refult of a truly meek and moral intellect, and I am told are excellently calculated to cherifh and cultivate fimilar difpofitions in the people. Profeffing myfelf, however, but little converfant in the Gentoo code, I fhall mention only a very few of their political inftitutions :— Whoever refufes to pay a tax impofed by the authority of the public, is liable to be charged with a double rate, but is never on this account fubjected to corporal punifhment, that being referved for the violations of man's natural rights : murder and affaffination are punifhed with death; feduction in either fex with the forfeiture of liberty, and the lofs of one eye; robbery with the amputation of one hand, and perpetual flavery;—thefe judicious laws render it very feldom neceffary for the magiftrate to exact penalties of a fanguinary nature.   The

principle

principle of the political and moral regula‑
tions of the Bramins is to allure man to his
native innocence and fimplicity, to engage
him to conform his actions to the firft principles of his nature, and efpecially to abftain
from whatever may have a tendency to ir-
ritate or inflame his paffions. This is the
great object of the divine law; and fhould
the wifdom of man try to accomplifh
more, the experiment will unavoidably
fail. I am likewife of opinion that the
claffing men in different cafts is an infti-
tution formed to produce the moft pure
and genuine manners.

Many of the obfervations I made in the
ifland Samar I found not only applicable
to this country, but even illuftrated and
confirmed by the lives of the Bramins,
men whom, except in matters of religious
opinion, I was in all refpects ambitious to
imitate. Like my neighbour Bramin, my
refidence was in the midft of a large and
beautiful garden, in which my hours glid-
ed fmoothly on in one quiet and uniform
tenor. Rice, fruit, and vegetables, gather-
ed and dreffed with my own hands, a diet

to

to which my ſtomach had been long ac-
cuſtomed, adminiſtered to my daily ſubſiſ-
tence.   My travels had given occaſion to
an extreme heat of blood, an indiſpoſition
I was at pains to remove by drinking rice-
broth, which, properly dreſſed, is equally
palatable with the fineſt milk.   Two pieces of cotton cloth, the one a covering to
my loins, and the other thrown over my
ſhoulders, compoſed my ordinary dreſs.   I
allowed my beard to grow in imitation of the
higheſt caſt, and like them generally walked
abroad with my head uncovered and my
feet bare.   In ſituations of any ceremony
I appeared in my full dreſs, which con-
ſiſted in a long white robe girt round the
waiſt in the manner of the Marrattas; and
with a turban and ſandals, in the Mooriſh
faſhion.   My time was employed chiefly in
reading, walking, and cultivating my garden.   A few goats and ſome poultry,
which I found means to procure in the
neighbourhood, contributed to my amuſement; and I occaſionally made viſits in
the adjacent villages.   Agreeably to the
manners of the country, I paſſed the night

on a mat of reeds, whofe cool and temperate effect afforded me the moft falutary and refrefhing repofe.

This courfe of life, which I purfued with much fatisfaction for a confiderable time, was fo analogous to the manners of the Gentoo, and fo different from thofe of an European, that it foon procured me the credit and reputation of a moft fincere penitent. The Bramin, as well as the Chriftian, began to regard me with an eye of veneration. I was vifited, invited to all entertainments, and every body feemed ambitious of my acquaintance. I received prefents of the choiceft fruits from the neighbouring gardens; and, in fhort, came to be efteemed a moft devout man, who was employed in expiating his fins by the rigorous aufterities of a new life. But, alas! my virtues were far from meriting the high encomiums they received; and I was in the painful and humiliating fituation of a man who muft hear himfelf praifed for certain good or great qualities, which he is inwardly confcious he does not pofiefs.

VOL. II.   E   I had

I had the misfortune to be feized with a diforder named fernas, pretty common in this country, which is accompanied with large puftules on the body and hands. Thofe on the fingers occafioned me the lofs of four of my nails. At the end of twenty days, after having tried various remedies in ufe among the people, finding myfelf ftill greatly indifpofed, I fet out for Surat, hoping to receive more benefit from the medical fkill of the capital. The fatigue of the journey, change of air, and, above all, the advantage of fea-bathing, difcharged my pimples; and I began to find myfelf confiderably better.

Five months had now elapfed fince I came to refide in the country, during which period I went frequently abroad, and made excurfions in all directions, without meeting with the fmalleft danger. The civil reception I every where experienced from the inhabitants, I am inclined to impute partly to my complexion, which fatigue and the influence of hot climates had rendered fimilar to their own, and partly to my drefs, which was entirely accommodated

dated to the taſte of the natives. The
only language in which I could make my-
ſelf underſtood was that of the Portugueſe,
which, though ſomewhat in uſe in the
country, is far from being generally ſpo-
ken; hence, on various occaſions, I was
taken for a Hindoo. In all ſituations,
however, I was equally the object of confidence and hoſpitality. It is evident, the
crimes of theft and robbery muſt be extremely rare, ſince, in the courſe of ſo
many months, a ſingle inſtance of either
did not come within the compaſs of my
knowledge; and though I was on different
occaſions three or four days from home,
when, according to the cuſtom of the
country, the door of my cottage was left
open, I never had the ſlighteſt reaſon to
ſuppoſe that a ſtranger had croſſed the
threſhold in my abſence.

In thoſe countries, I have obſerved,
where the people are nearly upon a foot-
ing in point of property, the private rights
of individuals are leaſt liable to be in-
vaded; for, by this means, a certain de-
ſcription of evil propenſities, which grow

E 2   out

out of arbitrary diftinctions, and increafe in violence with the unequal diftribution of property, are evidently precluded.

I was at Pardy the day of the carnival of the Gentoos who, on this occafion run about the ftreets, dufted over in their faces and cloaths with powder of different colours. Dancing to every inftrument of noife, and imparting to all who come in their way the fame ridiculous appearance with themfelves, feemed to be the chief objects of their amufement. Next day I lodged at Naufary, in the gardens of a rich Perfian, who, in the true fpirit of hofpitality, has erected a magnificent tent in the midft of a beautiful parterre, for the reception and entertainment of ftrangers. On the enfuing day, being the 19th March, I arrived at Surat, and alighted at the French factory. I embraced the conful's obliging offer of accommodation in his family; and waited a whole month for the failing of a Moorifh veffel, which an eminent merchant of Surat was equipping for the trade of Baffora. By this means I had an opportunity

tunity of obtaining a more perfect knowledge of this harbour, by far the moft confiderable in the poffeffion of the natives.
The commerce of European nations in
India was formerly confined to a few factories at this port; and I am of opinion,
it would have been fortunate for both
parties had there exifted in convenient fituations on the Indian coaft, other fuch
confiderable cities as Surat. The power
of the Indian princes, in thefe circumftances, would have operated with more effect, and might have checked that fpirit
of conqueft in Europeans, which, partly
owing to the calamities infeparable from war,
but chiefly to the fad diminution it occafions in the induftry of the people, muft always prove difaftrous to the proper views of
a trading company. The commerce of
Canton has been uniformly carried on
nearly upon the fame terms with all nations whatever; and ftill the Chinefe trade
continues to maintain its ground in a manner advantageous both to the native and
foreigner, a fact which I confider as an il-

E 3 luftration

luftration and proof of the truth of my opinion.

Surat ftands in a large and fertile plain, with few trees, particularly on the left fide of the river, and commands a view of the oppofite grounds. The ftreets are of confiderable breadth; but aukwardly formed, miferably paved, and, from the various induftry of a crouded population, extremely inconvenient. The houfes are large and ftrong buildings, in good tafte, and well fuited to the climate; though with very little outwardly to recommend them. The public markets of every denomination are well fupplied with all the neceffaries and comforts of life. The incredible number of flaves and fepoys, it being competent to every individual to have as many armed men in his fervice as he can afford to pay; and the conftant repair of coaches and palanquins, imprefs the mind of a ftranger with a high idea of the affluence of the people. The cabriole, but in the Moorifh tafte, is as common at Surat as is that vehicle in the ftreets of London or Paris; and, as it is drawn by oxen trained to go

at

at a gallop, is equally convenient and expeditious: the pole and ftraps of the carriage are of bamboo, and have all the elafticity of our main-braces. The gardens are many and beautiful. The harbour is greatly frequented; and the fhips built in their dock-yards are of a ftrong and folid conftruction. The trade of Surat, ftill very extenfive, has, however, been much impaired by certain impolitic regulations introduced by the nabob, at the inftigation of the Englifh.

This being the great mart for the immenfe produce of one of the richeft and moft extenfive parts of India, the quantity and variety of merchandize difplayed in the warehoufes are aftonifhing to a ftranger. Befides the European factories, there are here numbers of Moorifh, Perfian, and Gentoo merchants; and, in order that the reader may have an idea of a merchant of Surat, I fhall juft mention the proprietor of the fhip on board of which I had taken a paffage for Baffora. His trade, it is proper to obferve, had decreafed to lefs than one half of what it had been formerly; but

E 4

he

he was ftill owner of ten large armed veffels, which he lets out in freight to the
Englifh. From his flaves he obtains agents
and fupercargoes for his factories abroad,
and fometimes captains and officers for the
veffels he equips and employs on his own
account. His fhips, as well as his factory
at Baffora, difplay his flag; and he poffeffes in fovereignty a confiderable ifland in
the Euphrates. His commercial opera-
tions extend over the whole Indian coaft,
from China to Baffora. In his family are
at leaft a hundred flaves of fome diftinction,
who have flaves under them. I faw him
on a day of unufual ceremony, when he
appeared mounted on an elephant, and,
befides a long train of dependants on foot,
was attended by a numerous company of
his own relations on horfeback, and in
palanquins. Two hundred of his fepoys
led the van, while a large collection of mu-
fical inftruments, braying intolerable dif-
fonance, clofed the rear; a proceffion
which, in my opinion, would have better
fuited the emperor of Java than a dealer
in callicoes at Surat.

I attended

I attended the commemoration of Abraham's facrifice, or the Courbanbeyran, a folemnity to which the extraordinary pomp of the Indian grandees in their attendance on the nabob to his mofque, the incredible number of troops, the bands of mufic, the fplendour of equipages and robes, and the immenfe croud of fpectators affembled from all quarters, gave peculiar grandeur and magnificence. His highnefs was efcorted by five or fix thoufand fepoys, and a confiderable train of artillery, whilft between him and his mufti the Englifh counfellors, with a body of the company's troops, took diftinguifhed precedence.

Here it is fometimes difficult to fay in which of thefe powers, the Englifh, the Marrattas, or the nabob, the fupreme authority is vefted ; hence, in the courfe of my travels, I have never met with fuch numbers of armed men in any other city in the world. The Englifh are in poffeffion of the caftle and certain gates, the nabob is nominally mafter of the city, and the Marrattas, who claim a kind of tribute annually from the inhabitants, have two gates and a large body of troops ; but, from this aukward collifion of divided authority, there frequently arifes much public violence and diforder. I conclude thefe obfervations on Surat, the grandeur of which, though in a ftile extremely different from all that I have ever feen of the fame kind in Europe, contains, however, fomething peculiarly magnificent, and impofing on the imagination.

C H A P. III.

Voyage from Surat to Baffora, Mafcate in Arabia Felix, Bender Aboucheir in Perfia; my Abode at Baffora.

ON the 20th of April we fet fail for Baffora, in company with an armed Englifh veffel, which ferved us for a pilot and convoy to the mouth of the gulph. She was deftined to fcour the coafts of the *Sindys* and *Chamchas*, not of Marratta pirates, as is commonly fuppofed. The good government of the Marratta tribes, and particularly their unremitting induftry to reprefs the progrefs of piracy in thofe feas, by means of forts and cruizers, to which even the Portuguefe flag owes its protection, render it extremely improbable that the

the freebooters who moleft the Malabar
coaft, and who are generally called Marratta pirates, actually belong to thofe
ftates. It is poffible, indeed, that they
defcend from the fouthern parts of the
Marratta dominions; but in this cafe, un-
owned and unencouraged by that government, they fkulk under the flag of little
difaffected princes, who are very frequent
on thofe coafts.

Being to touch at Mafcate, and as the
S. W. winds were faft approaching, and
the direction of the current bore towards
the coaft of Sindys or Diu, we fteered
weftward, and made land on a low and
fandy fhore, S. W. of the Refulgat mountains. We then coafted northward, and
dropped anchor at Mafcate, after a paffage
of thirteen days. Befides a large and excellent road, there is here a very good harbour, in which we found four fathom and
a half of water. The high mountains of
the coaft and adjacent iflands, by which
the harbour is formed, cover it from the
winds, and protect it in all feafons from the
inconvenience of a rolling fea. S. W. from

the

the heights of cape Refulgat, and on that
part of the coaft where we went on fhore,
is another port; but it is only frequented
by the Arabs, the Abyffinians, and the
trade of the Red Sea. Mafcate is without the ftreights of Ormus, and confequently in a moft favourable fituation for
trade. Hence it ferves as an emporium
for the commerce of Indus, whofe ftreights
are liable to be frequently rough and tem-
peftuous; as well as for that of the Perfian
gulph, whofe navigation is much more tedious and uncertain than that of the Indian
fea.

Our pilot, though an Indian moor, was
a man of good capacity; he fettled with
great facility the fhip's courfe, but by rules
different from ours, which I cannot pretend to explain: he gave his orders with
much compofure and precifion; and guid-
ed the veffel by charts, which he himfelf
had drawn of the Chinefe gulph of Ben-
gal and Perfia. Had the natural talents of
this Moor been cultivated by the fcience of
mathematics, and had he poffeffed in a
higher degree the enterprize of a European
navigator,

navigator, I am fatisfied he would have made an excellent feaman.

I took the earlieft opportunity of going afhore, and met with a native of Hifpahan who acted as agent for French affairs in this city. The Arabian populace have generally been reprefented as a wicked and licentious race of men; a report which, as I went about in town and country, in an European drefs, without meeting with the fmalleft difturbance, my own experience by no means warrants me to confirm. In this town, which, by the bye, is miferably built, I faw a number of fine gardens; befides trefoil, and as many vegetables as a fcanty foil, lying among barren rocks, may be expected to produce, there are here dates, apricots, and fig-trees, both of India and Europe. They have roots and vegetables equal to the confumption of the inhabitants as well as ftrangers. This port is frequented by fhipping from the different countries of India; but particularly by fuch as are employed in the coafting trade from Eleatif all the way to Ceylon. The quiet manners of the Arabians in this city,

city, are probably owing to their intercourfe
with ftrangers, to their being accuftomed
to mingle with people of all religions, as
well as to the good policy of the Iman or
fovereign, who is anxious to promote the
interefts of trade and navigation in every
part of his dominions. Befides, it is ftill
recollected that this country once belonged to the Portuguefe, and that forcible
means have occafionally been employed to
controul the reftlefs humour of the natives; and hence the reafon, I prefume,
why Europeans experience a degree of
confideration here, which they do not enjoy in any other part of Arabia. The Iman
is too fenfible to the advantages of their
commerce, to difcourage their entering his
harbour; but he is alfo jealous of their conduct, and too cautious of his own fecurity
to permit them to fettle in his town.   He
knows, that although Mafcate is fituated
on the mainland of Arabia, it is, however,
in a manner infulated from the continent
by very high and inacceffible mountains,
and therefore trembles at the thought of
admitting an European colony within the
† 						walls

walls of a city, which has no communication with his other dominions, except by a narrow pafs among fteep and rugged rocks, where a handful of men might eafily ftop the progrefs of a whole army.

The Iman of this kingdom affects to be the only real defcendant of Mahomet, and therefore wears a blue inftead of the green turban, which is worn by the cheiks of Turky. He is fovereign of an extenfive country, and refides in his capital, fituated behind lofty and arid mountains, at five days journey from Mafcate. Paffing the mountains of Mafcate, the traveller defcends into a vaft plain covered with date trees, interfperfed with herds of cattle and fruitful fields, and cultivated by a people of civil and obliging manners. Such is the information, at leaft, which I received from a French factor, who, in order to avoid the heat of Mafcate, which the reflection of the mountains, and the fcarcity of rain in the dry feafon, render almoft uninhabitable, is ufed to pafs the fummer months in that country. Rain never falls oftener in this part of the world than four, or perhaps five times in the year.

In

In thofe regions the bulk of the inhabitants live chiefly on dates and milk, con-
verted into a very dry fubftance, with the
appearance of little flint ftones; which,
however, being again diffolved, affords a
kind of acid, but refrefhing liquor. The
environs of Mafcate, which are extremely
confined by their contiguity to thefe high
naked mountains, produce nothing but a
fmall quantity of vegetables. From the fea
coaft, however, they are well fupplied in
fifh, while all other articles neceffary for
fubfiftence are imported either by fea from
Sindys and Perfia, or upon the backs of mules
from the interior parts of the country.

I obferved both at Batavia and Surat,
that the Afiatic women, efpecially Mahometan, appear very feldom abroad. At
Surat, the perfons as well as faces of the
fex are covered with a veil; but at Mafcate thefe oriental manners are obferved
with fuch extreme rigour, that not even in
a fhop or public market is an Arabian female to be feen. During my abode in
this city I did not obferve an individual of
the moft amiable part of our fpecies, three
negroes

negroe flaves excepted, and they were wrapped up in large linen cloaks.

Having fpent feveral days at this port, one of the moft commercial in Arabia Felix, we got a pilot for the Perfian Gulph, and after weighing anchor ftood for the Streights of Ormus: we came in view of them in the fpace of two days; but as the wind blew from the N. W. frefh and fqually, in order to clear the ifles of Ormus and Mamouth Salem we were obliged to keep tacking for feveral days.

The terror of a high rolling fea prevalent in the Streights of Ormus, has given rife to a very fingular cuftom practifed by the Indian mariners. On a certain day of the year they conftruct, as a prefent for and in order to appeafe the wrath of Mamouth Salem, a fmall veffel, which upon entering the Streights they launch into the waves, fatisfied that by this fymbolical fhipwreck they elude the fury of that vengeance which was pointed againft themfelves. To this rite of fuperftition fucceeds a mock naval engagement, in which the brave exertions of the natives to defend the entrance to

their feas againft the invafions of the enemy, are meant to be reprefented; when the
former, after difplaying many feats of heroic
valour, are conftantly victorious.

We foon difcovered a cape on the coaft
of Perfia, which forms a kind of elbow, and
determines the entrance to the Streights.
I had been told it was ufual to fail immediately round it; but our pilot was of a different opinion, and chofe to ftand towards
the other fide, keeping at feveral leagues
diftance from the coaft of Arabia. I cannot, however, give him much credit for his
ability as a feaman on this occafion, for
next day the wind fhifted to the N. W.
and blew frefh with violent fqualls; we
were now therefore in the feafon when
the N. W. winds prevail in the Perfian
Gulph, and as they continue to blow during the fummer months, the paffage of
the Streights was become extremely precarious. We entered the Sound, which continues all the way to Baffora; and having
difcovered the coaft of Bender Abaffy, a port
much frequented in former times, we ftood
along the fide of a little ifland fituated S.
W.

W. of *Camron* or *Kifmifh*, between which two places lies a paffage into the Streights. The wind favouring us a little, we coafted the ifland *Camron* on the fide next the fea. As we advanced the courfe of the current, which iffues from the mouth of the gulph, as well as the N. W. wind, which kept blow-ing all the way to Baffora, were againft us. We failed, therefore, at the diftance of only five or fix leagues from the coaft of Perfia, in order to keep as much as poffible in the line of feparation between the N. W. wind which blows towards the coaft of Arabia, and is efteemed extremely unwholefome, and that ftormy region which lies along the Perfian fhore. We had at times favourable intervals, and continuing the fame courfe we left three iflands towards the coaft of Ara-bia, but kept conftantly at the fame dif-tance from the fide of Perfia, being ap-prehenfive of meeting with ftorms or calms under the adjacent mountains.

I lived on the beft terms with our Moorifh paffengers, whofe meek and peaceable difpofitions harmonized with my own. They appeared fomewhat fana-

F 2

tical

tical in matters of religion, as indeed are all Muſſulmen of great towns, but I was careful to give them no offence in their exerciſes, for while they ſaid prayers and read the *Coran* at my ſide, I made it my buſineſs never to be found between their proſtrations and the prophet's grave at Mecca. Their complaiſant behaviour was not confined to Muſſulmen, but extended equally to Gentoos, Chriſtians, and Jews, a liberality which ſoftened in ſome degree the harſh opinion I had been uſed to entertain of all who had imbibed the haughty and imperious doctrines of Mahomet. The firſt principles of that law, though ſevere and intolerating as to manners, are in many reſpects juſt; but their ſyſtem being upon the whole a tranſcript of the prejudices and narrow character of its founder, tends to inculcate on the minds of its votaries a ſuperlative notion of high ſuperiority over other men. The friendly and ſociable behaviour, therefore, of theſe Moors, I would refer partly to the native character of the Aſiatic, and partly to the beſt maxims and inſtitutions of their religion.

We

We had likewife twenty dervifes, whofe deportment was in every refpect congenial to their profeffion, and engaged my fincere veneration. From their converfation I could difcover in thefe men the foundeft principles of morality, which their painful fituation on this voyage gave them frequent occafion to exercife. One of their companions lay on his death-bed, a man, who after fuffering extreme agony, which he bore with great conftancy and refignation, fhewed in the peculiarly mild and ferene effect of his countenance at the moment of his diffolution, with how little regret he bade adieu to this frail and miferable body. For the edification of the company during our meals, the beft informed among the dervifes were regularly invited by the fhip's officers to read and explain certain paffages of their books; but thefe lectures I ufed to find of a very tirefome length. On fuch occafions I enjoyed the agreeable fociety of a Jew, a native of Aden, who was not inferior to any of our paffengers in the meek and moral virtues of the Afiatic; and with whom I had much fatisfaction in difcuf-

fing

fing the grounds of our different religious opinions.

The ſhip's officers ſeemed to be of an inquiſitive diſpoſition, and hence, among many other queſtions, I was aſked, why the French in general were ſo little addicted to the ſame ſimple manner of thinking and acting as my-ſelf; whence that extreme impatience of their native country, which hurried them to the ends of the earth, amaſſing money, and ſpending it to no manner of purpoſe; and what pleaſure or amuſement they could find in being the inſtruments of animoſity and diſſenſion in all thoſe nations which had the misfortune of their viſits? They expreſſed much regret that the Europeans had been ſo ſuccefsful in ſeducing the natives of Aſia to their intereſts and views, the pernicious effects of which they alledged were now felt, when it was too late to remedy them. I talked a great deal of the glory of the *Grande Monarque,* and the dignity as well as ſecurity of the ſtate: but they could entertain no notion of glory, or even of duty, when ſeparated from moral rectitude, and the principles of a ſimple and charitable mind.

mind. I will not pretend to fay which opinion prevailed in point of argument; but it was evident, that though they feemed extremely candid and open to information, I had not the honour to bring them over to my fide of the queftion.

The Afiatics in general confider Europeans as men of reafoning, rather than reafonable men; or in other words, as a race of ingenious fools; and in this opinion our whole fhip's company feemed to concur. According to them, in order to form a right judgment of any thing, a man fhould affume the character of a judge, divefting himfelf of all bias and intereft whatever with regard to the point in difcuffion. He muft poffefs the faculty of a juft and luminous underftanding, with what they term an unimpaired elafticity of brain, requifites feldom to be found in a man of bufinefs, the bent of whofe ideas is too much directed towards one object, and never, they contend, to be found in an European, whofe prejudiced habits of life are wholly incompatible with freedom of reflection and found judgment. The reafoning of thefe people

F 4 did

did not appear to me to be altogether in the wrong; but when I confidered their indolence, and our weaknefs, probably the difference between us is only in degree; for it is impoffible that human candour and impartiality fhould ever reach fo high a ftandard, as that all the fentiments of even the beft men fhall be true, and exactly conformable to the nature of things.

Although thefe men were by no means adepts in the fcience of geometry, they affected to afcertain the feat of juft thought by a very fingular kind of mathematical illuftration. This, they fay, is to be found on the vertex of a very obtufe angle, formed by two lines, the extremities of which at the point of contact reprefent fenfe and reafon. The other extremities of the lines, on account of the fpecies of angle they contain, are almoft oppofite to each other, and denote folly in oppofition to fenfe, and ftupidity in oppofition to reafon;—now the moment a man recedes from the angular point where fenfe and reafon are united, and where nature originally placed him, he begins to approximate the extreme, either

ther

ther of folly or ftupidity. In their application of this problem, the natives of
both countries deal uncandidly with each
other; for while the Afiatic finds the European at the pinnacle of folly, the European is equally fure he difcovers the Afiatic
in the extreme point of ftupidity. For
my part, I am perfuaded that neither
the one nor the other is in a condition to
mantain his balance on the angular point.
And therefore to man, liable as he is to be
furprized and agitated by all the violent
paffions of his nature, the ftation affigned
him by the Indian philofopher muft ever
afford us a precarious fupport.——But I
return to the fequel of my voyage.

We touched at Bender Abouchier, a fea
port of Perfia, where after executing the
inftructions of our employers, we were to receive a new pilot. The firft pilot belonged
to Mafcate, and had engaged to conduct us
for fifty rupees only to Abouchier; but
befides, we were now to enter the channel
of the Euphrates, the navigation of which
this pilot did not pretend to underftand,
it was plain he was but a novice in the
practical

practical part of his profeſſion, for at the
diſtance of twenty leagues from Abouchier
the ſhip got entangled among rocks,
which project from a certain cape far into
the ſea, whereby we were conſiderably detained.   While we were ſtruggling with
our difficulties amidſt theſe rocks at leaſt
five leagues from land, the wind, conſtantly
in the N. W, ſprung up freſh and ſqually,
and we were obliged to drop an anchor in
twenty fathoms water, two leagues from
the ſhore.   It having calmed, we again
got under weigh, and at length doubled the
cape, after which the coaſt begins to recede
towards the N. E,; but we ſpent twelve
days in recovering the advantage we had
loſt by the inexperience of our pilot.   We
now ſtood with the rocks of the cape on our
right, and a ſmall iſland with ſeveral adjacent ſand-banks on the larboard ſide. Theſe
rocks are very ignorantly laid down on our
charts, which indeed are in general extremely inaccurate reſpecting the navigation of this gulph.   Six days after, as we
paſſed a fort, formerly in poſſeſſion of the
Portugueſe we began to enter the road of
Abouchier,

Abouchier, which is much expofed to the weather, but has an excellent bottom.

In the mouth of the port lay a veffel belonging to Great Britain, which is the only European nation feen here in the purfuits of trade. The entrance to the harbour being formed by banks of fand, which extend a great way into the gulph, is extremely difficult of accefs; befides, the road is at too great a diftance from land, and the coaft is exceffively low towards the edge of the fea.

From this plentiful country, which is regarded as the granary of Baffora, we received an excellent fupply of provifions. The foil immediately about Baffora, as well as the adjacent country, being miferably dry and barren, its inhabitants are indebted for the neceffaries of life to Bender Abouchier, whofe environs are remarkably fertile and pleafant.

Having taken on board a pilot for the further profecution of our voyage, in confideration of whofe trouble and the ufe of a founding boat we were to pay thirty rupees, we again put to fea with a favourable

able wind, and ftood for the mouth of
the Euphrates.   We had failed little more
than three leagues and a half, for we
had not yet doubled the ifland of Careith,
when the wind returning to the N. W.
blew frefh, and exceffively hot.   We tack-
ed, but without gaining the fmalleft advantage; and the wind continuing to
blow with the fame force, feconded by
the current; and our water, of which we
had laid in none at Abouchier, beginning to
fail; we came to anchor at Careith.   The
fovereignty of this ifland, I find, belongs to
a Perfian chief, who pays tribute to the
prince of Bender Abouchier.   This prince
likewife receives tribute from the little ifland
of Barheim, famous for its pearl-fifheries.
The empire of Perfia, like that of the
Mogul, is broken into fmall principalities,
which are held and acknowledged by their
refpective lords as fiefs under the prince
of Hifpahan.

The ifle of Careith, which once belonged to the Dutch, and which the Englifh in a
later period endeavoured to become mafters
of, is at prefent inhabited by Perfians, Curds,
and

and Arabs, who all agree in one point,
viz. a moft rooted antipathy to Europeans. The Careith veffels, which infeft the
Perfian Gulph are like our gallies; and
though they are fcarce confidered in the light
of pirates, every European trader ought to be
well armed and in condition to face them.
Prefuming at firft fight that we belonged to fome European port, they gave chace,
and ftopped our fhip's boat; but upon dif-
covering we were Indian it was releafed,
and we were permitted to profecute our
voyage.

The inhabitants of Abouchier itfelf are
far from being in the intereft of Europeans,
and hence the bottom of the gulph from
Barheim to Abouchier is frequented by a
number of fmall veffels, a fort of femi-
pirates, againft which fuch fhips from
Europe as have bufinefs in thefe feas would
do well to be on their guard. Though
we had been provided in a pilot for the Euphrates at Abouchier, we were obliged to
hire another at Careith; and as a part of
his falary is a perquifite to government,
it was idle to infift upon the inutility

of

of two pilots for the fame voyage. Having
therefore, according to Afiatic cuftom, made
him a prefent over and above his wages, and
received another in return, we again fet fail.
As this coaft lies extremely low, and is bordered all along with flooded grounds, and
having a moft unfkilful pilot, it was with
great difficulty, and by conftantly heaving the
lead, that we at laft reached the mouth of
the river.   At the diftance of eight leagues
from the Euphrates, our pilots, I obferved, became anxious about what they
called the entrance to the old bed of the
river, which is fituated on the Curd coaft.
We paffed over various banks and gutters,
along which the river difcharges itfelf into
the gulph, and were twice a-ground, notwithftanding the attention of our pilots, before we could reach the coaft of Arabia. We
fent the boat and fome of our hands on
fhore, in order to difcover if they could
the date-tree; for as it is not produced
on the confines of the other paffages, it is
by this means they are enabled to afcertain
the principal canal of the river.   We were
foon prefented with a date branch, which

I   encourag-

encouraged our pilots, and they entered boldly into the channel. As this paffage runs in a line parallel to the fhore, as foon as the veffel gets fight of land, which, however, is extremely low, fhe is known to be clear of all thofe banks that incommode the navigation of the Euphrates. Befides the inconvenience of a very rapid current, there is but twenty feet water at flood tide in the deepeft of thofe channels, which run between the fand-banks formed in the bed of the river. It is neceffary in thofe narrow canals to be particularly careful not to run a-ground; for, being expofed in this fituation to the whole force of the current, the veffel would be in danger of going to pieces. When the pilot is apprehenfive, therefore, of fuch an accident, he endeavours to lay the fhip in a cavity of the bank: as the force of the current has been already broken in its defcent, fhe may remain in tolerable fafety.

The Curd coaft being formed entirely of funk grounds, I am inclined to believe that the other paffages up the Euphrates, mentioned by fome navigators, are extremely

tremely narrow; at leaft, I can fay that in
failing up this river I did not find, and I
have not heard that there is any other very
confiderable canal.

The dry and fandy coaft of Arabia is the
certain mark of the branch we purfued; but
we had fteered along this coaft a confiderable
time, when we arrived at the extremity of
the river's oppofite bank, which is on the
Curd fide, greenifh, and ought to be in view
before the pilot attempts to enter into the
middle of the channel. The veffel no fooner
gets between the banks of the Euphrates,
than the depth of water is found to be confiderably increafed. As Baffora is at the
diftance of forty leagues from the fea, fhips
mount with the tide, and drop anchor at
Jufan in any place they pleafe, unmolefted
by the current. At Jufan the bottom is
good, and of a greenifh clay, but of fo tenacious a quality, that it is often difficult
to weigh anchor: all the way for about
twenty-five leagues from the mouth of
the river, it is tolerably neat and clean,
but there it begins to be incommod-
ed

ed by fand-banks, which render this navigation very difficult.

The Euphrates detaches, on the fide of Arabia, a fmall canal navigable for boats of fifty tons, along which are villages that trade with Baffora, and El'catif, a town of Arabia, fituated in the line of the canal. We continued our courfe along the coaft of Arabia; but found it neceffary to proceed with the greateft circumfpection, particularly where the fhore is low, as it is fometimes without date-trees, and covered with water at high fea.

We paffed a mofque of dervifes on the Curd coaft, and afterwards the ruins of fome old fortifications, to which Solimancha, a famous Curd chieftain, made faft on each fide of the river chains and a bridge of boats, when he intercepted the navigation of the Euphrates. About fix leagues from Baffora, we paffed to the left of the little ifland of Cheliby, and afterwards difcovered, on the coaft of Arabia, the mouth of a fmall river, on the banks of which ftands an inconfiderable mofque. Here, at a third of the river's breadth from the Arabian coaft,

the Baffora fhipping come to anchor. On
the border of this river, and only a quarter
of a league within the extremities of its
banks, ftands the city of Baffora, whofe
gardens extend to the very edge of the
Euphrates.

Here we found three armed fhips belonging to Great Britain, which were deftined for the protection of the Englifh at
Baffora, Aboucheir, and Mafcate, as well
as to defend their trade from the depredations of the natives in the navigation of
the gulph. The Englifh poffefs the greateft part of the Baffora trade; but as the
Arabs and Curds, who compofe the bulk
of the inhabitants, are very little civilized,
and as the Turks, from their remote fituation from Europe, might be tempted to
expel ftrangers, with a view to a monopoly
of this trade, the Englifh have had the ad-
drefs, under various pretexts, to get five
hundred national troops ftationed on fhore.
Befides, as their fhips lie at anchor within
lefs than a gun-fhot of the town, they are
in condition to over-awe the inhabitants
upon any emergency that may render their
interference

interference expedient. The Arabian populace are generally confidered, as has been already obferved, fpiteful and vindictive to ftrangers, particularly Europeans; I have feen, however, Indian failors in the fervice of the Englifh give law to the natives of Baffora, by a fevere application of the oar. This behaviour would have been very differently received from the retainers of any other nation whatever; but it is a common obfervation, that the arrogance of a powerful mafter often defcends to his fervant; hence, though naturally tame and unwarlike in his own character, he will affect a fuperiority over thofe who, on ordinary occafions, are much braver than himfelf. In the exercife of a moft extenfive commerce, the Englifh have difcovered the good policy of appearing open and liberal in their tranfactions with ftrangers; and therefore, though their conduct, in other refpects, often gives umbrage, they are efteemed as merchants.

Baffora is a large and populous city; but the town-walls, as well as private houfes, which are poor habitations, are built en-

tirely

tirely of earth. The houfes are either altogether without windows, or have them of a very fmall fize, in order to exclude the burning winds of the defert, which commences under the walls of the town. The banks of the Euphrates fupply the inhabitants with fruit and vegetables, while they receive from Bender Aboucheir all the other neceffaries of life. The bulk of the people, like the reft of the natives in this quarter of Arabia, fubfift almoft entirely on dates and a kind of four milk. The cuftoms of the Eaft, refpecting the fex, obtain here in all their ftrictnefs; infomuch that, from the condition of children to that of full-grown women, they are equally invifible to the eye of a ftranger as if they were entirely extinct.

Baffora holds, under the Grand Signior, of the Bafha of Bagdad, who, however, poffeffes but a very limited authority, and finds it expedient to exercife much difcretion in his conduct towards both the Curds and Arabians. There are here feveral Jewifh and Arabian merchants, who trade with Aboucheir, Mafcate, Barheim, and Elcatif, efpecially

efpecially with the ifle of Barheim, which
fupplies the Elcatif merchants, as well as
thofe of the towns on the canal above-
mentioned, with beautiful pearls.

In the regions of the defert immediately contiguous to this city are cheiks
or Arabian chieftains, who entertain a
violent averfion to the Mahometans, and
who adore one God, without regard to
myftery, or any fyftematic form of worfhip whatever. The other inhabitants in
thofe parts, particularly on the confines of
the defert, are rigid followers of the prophet; but I am told, in the more central
regions there are feveral ignorant tribes,
half Jews and half Chriftians, who adhere
to no defined clafs of religious opinions in
the world.

Having quitted the fhip before fhe arrived at her ftation, I got on fhore the 25th
June 1770, and was well received by the
French conful, who politely made me
a tender of his fervices. Learning that
fifteen days before a very rich and numerous
caravan fet out for Aleppo, I faw with
much regret that our tedious paffage from

G 3   Surat

Surat had deprived me of an excellent opportunity of crossing the desert; and was
extremely apprehensive that I might be
obliged to wait six months at Bassora for
the departure of another. The merchants
of this place carry on a considerable traffic,
by means of large boats decked with lea-
ther, deep in the hull, and built of the
date-tree, (which is the only thing like
timber in this country) with all that part of
Asia under the dominion of the Porte which
communicates with the Tygris and Euphrates.

The industry of the people is observable
in a species of curious little boats, which
they equip for the navigation of the river.
They are of an oval form, made of osiers
interwoven in the manner of a basket, and
coated with mud and tar. They are very
properly named *couffes*, and move by means
of a kind of oar or scull, presenting a mode
of navigation which I had scarce met with
before.

My fears of being long detained at this
stage of my travels were of short continuance; for, agreeably to information I had
received

received at Surat, I was told the day after my arrival, that a caravan of Bedoüins, or Arabian shepherds, on their way to Aleppo with young camels, were encamped two day's journey from Baffora. Upon the caravan's halting in the neighbourhood, their chief had fent to make enquiry in the city whether there were any paffengers who defired to take the advantage of his protection over the defert. Some Arabians in the vicinity embraced this opportunity of going to Aleppo, from one of whom the French conful was fo obliging as to hire me a dromedary, and to agree with him for the carriage of my water and effects, at the fame time ftipulating with another for his fervices as a cook. The Moorifh veffel not being come into port, I made all poffible hafte to fetch my things from on board, and to lay in fuch provifions as were neceffary for the journey. I dreffed myfelf in a Turkifh habit, and, having made my beft acknowledgments to my friend the conful for all his civilities, I took my leave and departed.

G 4　　　　C H A P.

C H A P. IV.

A Journey from Baffora to Damafcus, over the Deferts of Arabia.

I Had been three days at Baffora, when, on the 28th of June, I fet out to join the caravan of Bedouin fhepherds.   In the evening we put up at a built* village, where I met with the Arabian with whom the conful had made for me an agreement, and from whom I received a written obligation for my fafe conduct to Aleppo. He took me under his care with every mark of hofpitality, and my entertainment began to favour rather more of the fhepherd than town life.   Next day the brother of my Arabian friend having acquainted me that every thing was ready for our departure, I mounted a camel, for the firft time in my life, in company with eight Arabs.   We began our march, and

* In contradiftinction to the moveable habitations of the defert.

came

came up in the evening with our caravan,
near a Bedouin camp, confisting of Arabs
who fojourn in thefe parts. Our caravan
amounted to a hundred and fifty men, and
fifteen hundred young camels. The defert
feemed entirely covered with herds and
flocks of various denominations, belonging
to the Bedouins of the neighbouring camp.
The camels wander over the defert during
the day in fearch of food, but are accuftomed to join the camp in the evening,
each repairing to his mafter's tent, before
which he fquats down until morning.
From their milk and fleeces the Arab derives all the fimple neceffaries of life, food,
cloathing, and lodging.

The day following we began to fet forward on our journey, when the great extent of ground covered by the caravan afforded a very beautiful and entertaining
profpect. On the fecond day of our march
we paffed the ruins of an old caftle in
the vicinity of a well, out of which we
filled our bottles; and in two days more
we came to other wells, and overtook a
couple of Arabs mounted on affes.

After

After travelling four days more, we difcovered an Arabian encampment; and here,
in order to prevent my being diftinguifhed
from my companions, I put on an *abc* or
robe, with a handkerchief floating on my
head, in the ftyle of the defert; for hitherto
I had been clad in the Turkifh fafhion,
which is different from that of the Arabs,
particularly the Bedouins. The *abc* confifts of woollen ftuff, and compofes the
drefs of both fexes. Next the fkin is generally worn a white one of a fine quality,
over which are two others of a larger fize;
and while the uppermoft remains loofe and
flowing, the fecond is faftened about the
waift with a girdle. The latter is commonly
ftriped black and white; but the former
is for the greateft part entirely black. This
robe is of a very fimple form, and, in order
that the reader may have a diftinct idea of
it, he has only to conceive a fack as wide
as it is long, which, being flit length-
ways for the convenience of putting it on,
and paffing it over the head, with two
holes, one in each corner, to receive
the arms, will be an exact model of the
Arabian

Arabian *abc*. This is all the variety of
drefs that enters into the wardrobe of the
Arab; his perfon, however, is completely
covered, and his *abe* being of fo clofe a
texture as to be impenetrable to water, is
an excellent defence againft the rain; and,
as it is large enough to give free accefs to
the air, and denfe enough to repel the firft
blufh of the fun's rays, it is equally ufeful againft the burning heat of the defert. No perfons wear either breeches or
drawers, as is cuftomary in towns. On
the head of the male is an ample fized
handkerchief of filk and cotton, attached
by a large piece of cotton cloth, which,
after paffing twice round the head, falls
down upon the fhoulders, covering them
by its breadth. The ends of the handkerchief having been doubled down on the
mouth and nofe, are returned under the
fillet which binds it to the head, and in this
manner he endeavours to defend the cheft
and lungs againft the dangerous influence of
a moft formidably dry and parching wind.
The true Bedouin Arab never fhaves either
his head or beard; and his hair, difpofed

into

into ten or twelve treffes, floats carelefsly on his fhoulders. The head-drefs of the women is almoft the fame; and indeed one perceives very little difference between the drefs of the two fexes, except in the colour of the handkerchief, and the jewels employed to adorn the head of the female. The *abe* of the women ferves for a complete veil to the face, there being only fuch a fmall aperture for the eyes, as is neceffary for ufe; but in many parts of thefe deferts the Arabs of both fexes go entirely naked.

The Bedouins, with a degree of prudence not always equally vifible in their conduct, as will afterwards appear, leaving their camels deftined for the Aleppo market confiderably behind us, proceeded a quarter of a mile from the Arabian camp. One of our men now ran before, to requeft the friendfhip of the tribe, a requeft which is complied with almoft of courfe as foon as a ftranger has arrived within the lines of their encampment. It is granted, however, according to cuftom, under all the formalities of war; and therefore

therefore a party of their warriors ruſhing
inſtantly from the camp, ran full ſpeed
towards ours. The Bedouins diſmount-
ed from their dromedaries, and proceeded
with equal celerity to meet them, when
mingling with much apparent rage, each
holding his lance pointed againſt the
breaſt of his opponent, they exhibited a
mock fight, accompanied with loud ſhouts
on both ſides. We were ſoon introduced to the camp, when peace and good order were immediately reſtored. My companions were deſirous to have ſome traffic
in camels, and we ſojourned within their
lines two days and a half.

One day I went on a viſit to the Bedouin camp entirely alone, for my conductor,
either really or affecting to be afraid of
ſome diſagreeable adventure, declined his
attendance. About the diſtance of forty
paces from their tents I was accoſted by
a ſingle Arab, who deſired to know my
buſineſs. Having made him underſtand that
I was a ſtranger in the deſert, and that cu-
rioſity alone had led me this way, he ſa-
luted me with much civility, and conducting

ing me to his tent, as a mark of his hofpita‐
lity placed me in the uppermoft feat: he
was by profeffion a fmith, and had a little
furnace, which he heated with charcoal
obtained from the roots of brambles ga‐
thered in the defert; he had contrived to
piece four fkins in the form of a large
bladder, which receiving a conftant pref‐
fure from two of his children, ferved in
place of a bellows. This, like all the other
tents in the camp, was much longer
than broad, with a partition in the mid‐
dle: the firft apartment belonged to the
mafter of the family, while the fecond was
occupied by his wife and other females,
who were employed in dreffing wool. I
made it my bufinefs to examine their wells,
which I found to be nothing more than
large holes dug in the earth, without any
lining whatever, and in which the water
ftood at the depth of fix feet from the fur‐
face. One of the moft beautiful mares I
had ever feen was ftanding at the door of
a neighbouring tent, which I likewife took
the liberty to enter. Here I was extremely
well received by a good old Arab, who was

engaged

engaged in making bottles and troughs of
goat-fkins; every creature I met, even
to the mare and her foal, came to fmell
me. I proceeded to make the tour of
another circle of tents, and found them
all open to leeward, but fhut againft the
burning wind of the defert, which prevails fix months in the fame quarter. It
feemed to be the chief employment of this
little commonwealth to drefs goats hair, and
the wool of their fheep and camels. One
circumftance which furprized me not a
little, was the incurious and indifferent air
of the people, who, though they treated me
with civility, yet never once ftirred from
their feats at my approach. Their tents being open length-ways, I had an opportunity of obferving that an Arab's family is
remarkably populous. This liftlefs inattention, efpecially in children, always eager to
examine whatever has the appearance of
novelty, appeared to me to be extremely
fingular; and the more fo that ftrangers
are but feldom feen in this part of Arabia,
it being near the centre of the defert.

The whole property of an Arab confifts

in

in his herds and flocks; his horfes, but more efpecially his mares, which he confiders as much more valuable, are of great ufe to him in his excurfions, and particularly in the purfuits of war: he is eminently diftinguifhed as a horfeman, and much more fkilful in the management of that animal than the native of any other country. The Arabian horfe, which feeds only once a day, and even then makes but a fcanty meal, is at the fame time the fleeteft and moft abftemious animal in the world.

The camel is perhaps of no lefs confequence to his wandering mafter; he ferves to tranfport his family and property from one part of the defert to another, and is, befides, an article of traffic for grain and other neceffaries of life. When, in confequence of the extreme drought, his grafs begins to fail, or his well to be dried up, the Arab decamps, and goes in queft of water and pafture in lefs inhofpitable regions. The whole defert is covered with a fine fand mixed with gravel, which produces only a few brambles about a foot

and

and a half high, and a kind of grafs with a fingle ftalk, but which is never found incorporated in the manner of our green turf.

During the fummer months there rages in the plains of Arabia a N. W. wind, violently heated by the reflection of the fand; and in winter the fcorching heat of the S. E. is perhaps ftill more unfupportable. In this feafon the rays of the fun are fo powerful, that the human fkin becomes crifped, and the pores fo conftricted as to ftop the ordinary courfe of perfpiration. Hence the Arabian has been taught to interpofe a very denfe medium between his body and the folar rays, againft which an European winter drefs of the moft fubftantial fabric would oppofe but a flender defence : he doubles down a thick handerchief tied round the forehead, over his mouth and nofe, in order to prevent that moifture which is neceffary to the cheft and lungs from being entirely exhaufted ; he is obliged, however, to leave his eyes wholly unprotected, which fuffer the moft acute pain from the heat and violent

II reflec-

reflection of the fand, and which confequently become in an early period of life
greatly weakened and impaired.

As the general afpect of the defert is that
of a vaft plain terminated on all fides by
the horizon, in vain does the roving eye
of the traveller feek to reft on fome intervening object; and hence, after flitting over
a difmal wafte of grey fand and fcorched
brambles, it returns at laft, languid and fatigued, to enjoy a little relaxation in the variety of herds and other Arabian property
with which he is furrounded. A deep and
mournful filence reigns over the dreary
landfcape; no beaft, no bird, no fpecies of
infect, is feen to diverfify the fad uniformity of the fcene. In the whole extent
of Arabia Deferta I faw only four rabbits,
five or fix rats, three large, and feven or
eight fmall birds; befides, the laft were
in the vicinity of an inhabited country,
whilft the former were natives of a more
earthy foil than is eafily to be met with in
thofe regions.

This fpecies of rat is remarkably handfome, and of a breed very different from
any

any I had before met with: his eyes are
large and fprightly; the whifkers, fnout,
and brow, as well as the belly, paws, and
end of the tail, are white, whilft the other
parts of the body are covered with a long
neat fur of a yellow colour: the tail is rather fhort, thick, yellow, and pointed with
white. Some of them were killed, and, after
being roafted, eaten by the Arabs, who are
accuftomed to throw their fticks with furprifing dexterity againft whatever bird or
quadrupede happens to come in their way.

The fmall quantity of water found in
this vaft defert is extremely falt and bitter;
but the Arab is trained to the hardfhips,
and attached to the freedom of his native
plains. Inured to fatigue, and carelefs of
the conveniencies of a wealthier fituation,
he looks down on the effeminate plea-
fures of more temperate climates with
fcorn and contempt. Brave, proud, hofpitable, and enterprizing, he is true to all his
engagements; being conftantly expofed,
however, to the inroads of warlike tribes,
he is prone to fufpicion, and hence receives
all ftrangers whatever with arms in his

hands.

hands. The individuals of the fame tribe, even of the loweft condition, being regarded by the reft of the clan in the light of brothers, any injury done to one is received and refented as an infult offered to the whole. They are extremely cautious of engaging in an affair from which blood may be expected to enfue; but are proportionally forward to action, in contempt of every danger, when they have a caufe to avenge.

The Arab is unfortunate enough to imagine he has the fame right to interfere with the property of another, which he, in exercifing the offices of hofpitality with regard to his own, refigns to a ftranger, and in this fenfe may be faid to be a robber; but in no cafe can he be charged nationally with the character of an affaffin. From the combination of thefe and fuch virtues and prejudices feem to refult the ftrength and union of the Arabian tribes; and were their manners a little more humanized by the influence of Chriftian morality, I know no race of men whatever whofe character would bid fairer for happinefs,

pinefs, or be lefs liable to corruption. The
extreme barrennefs of their deferts, which
difcourages the ambition, and defends them
againft the yoke, of a conqueror, the cer-
tainty of fubfiftence, and the entire exclu-
fion of luxury, conftitute their great charter
to independance, and thofe undepraved and
fimple manners, by which they have always
been diftinguifhed.

His ftrong attachment to freedom makes
an Arab cautious of acknowledging any
authority in his chief, which he cannot
difcover to be expedient for the good of the
community; but at the fame time, being
frequently at war with his neighbours, he
is fenfible that there muft be one man, in
whofe difcretion on fuch occafions the national will ought to center, in order that
the tribe may take the field in a body, and
act with proper effect againft the enemy.
The bulk of Arabian tribes bear the name
of the primitive ftock whence they are
refpectively defcended, and have no other
appellation than that of his children;
hence the Arabs by whom I was accom-

H 3

panied were called Ben Halet, or the children of Halet.

They run with extraordinary fwiftnefs,
and are fingularly dexterous in the management of the lance, have large bones,
a deep brown complexion, perfons of an
ordinary ftature, but lean, mufcular, active,
and vigorous. The Bedouins fuffer their
hair and beards to grow; and, indeed,
among the Arabian tribes in general, the
beard is remarkably full and bufhy. The
Arab has a large ardent black eye, a long
face, features high and regular, and, as
the refult of the whole, a phyfiognomy
particularly ftern and fevere. This expreffion, meeting with our pre-conceived notion of his character, gives him an air
of great ferocity; upon a little acquaintance, however, his formidable afpect fet-
tles into fomething truly noble and manly.

The tribes which frequent the middle
of the defert have locks fomewhat crifped,
extremely fine, and approaching the woolly
hair of the negro: my own, during the
fhort period of my travels in thofe regions,
became

became more dry and delicate than ufual, and receiving little nourifhment from a checked perfpiration, fhewed a difpofition to affume the fame frizzled and woolly appearance : an entire failure of moifture, and the exceffive heat of climate, by which it was occafioned, feemed to be the principal caufes of thofe fymptoms; my blood was become extremely dry, and my complexion differed little at laft from that of a Hindoo or Arab. It is not my intention, however, to offer any theory relative to the ftrong influence climate may be fuppofed to have on the external appearance of the human frame.

Having confidered the Arab with much attention in his manners and principles of action, I cannot agree in the common opinion which makes a propenfity to robbery a natural ingredient in his character. I had the ftrongeft evidence, in various fituations, of the honefty and fidelity of my fellow-travellers : I faw them living as a little commonwealth on the moft friendly and fociable terms; nor, indeed, have I ever heard that an Arab would be

H 4.   guilty

guilty of theft or robbery againſt thoſe of his own tribe; his appetite for plunder is exerted, in concert with his clan, againſt entire ſtrangers, and always within the boundaries of the deſerts; in no ſhape whatever will an Arab invade the property of another man in a town or cultivated country; and hence robbery in him is plainly derived from a prejudice of education, a prejudice in all reſpects ſimilar to that of the ancient Romans, who regarded every tribe and race of men not in their 'alliance, as enemies to the republic.

The Arab pays a ſcrupulous regard to all his engagements with ſtrangers; and therefore the traveller, upon making him a certain gratification, in conſideration of being ſuffered to paſs unmoleſted, or upon receiving the protection of any individual Arab, who in this caſe, from their fraternal union, is conceived to repreſent the tribe, enjoys an entire exemption from the ordinary effects of Arabian prejudices to ſtrangers. In ſuch circumſtances a foreigner may croſs the deſerts with as little

apprehen-

apprehenſion of injuſtice from the natives, as he ever entertained in travelling a high road in his native country.

That the Arab's right to his deſerts is of a leſs perfect kind than that of other nations to the countries they reſpectively inhabit, is an argument that will hardly be maintained; ſince, if long and uninterrupted poſſeſſion, according to the legal maxims of every civilized people, founds the requiſites of dominion, it is evident his claim to the deſerts is much leſs liable to exception than that of any prince whatever to the domains of his crown. But is there a ſovereign or independent ſtate in the world which does not vindicate an excluſive right to all the uſes of its ſoil?—or is this a rule of juriſprudence, in which the Arab alone is excepted?—a prince deſtitute of authority even on his own eſtate, and who muſt patiently give way to ſtrangers paſſing at diſcretion over his grounds? To this right of abſolute dominion, however, he has never rigidly adhered; all he requires is a certain tribute or cuſtom, proportioned to the quantity of goods or merchandize

meant

meant to be tranſported over the deſerts; a cuſtom, beſides, which each individual in the tribe, as repreſenting the community, has authority to exact or diſpenſe with as he may ſee cauſe.

This title, veſted in every member of the clan, is of general notoriety; and therefore intelligent travellers take care to have an Arab in their company, for a pledge of peace and ſecurity againſt the moleſtation of his tribe.

Such is the political conſtitution of the deſert, and whoever conducts himſelf in conformity to it has nothing to dread from the depredations of the natives; but if men, acting from ignorance, or in contempt of Arabian manners, ſhall expoſe themſelves to be pillaged, they have no right to repreſent the Arabs as a people, without diſtinction or enquiry, in the odious colours of robbers and banditti.

The peculiar circumſtances of this country muſt, no doubt, often render it painful to the bodily feeling of the native; but his hardſhips are conſiderably counterbalanced by the ſweets of independence, and that brotherly confidence and affection

which

which unite him to his tribe in all its interefts and purfuits.

I muft own I never felt fo fenfibly as here, and in the wilds of America, the charms of that invaluable liberty which is the gift of the Creator, but which in great cities and highly civilized countries is almoft extinguifhed by the habits of luxury, and the miferable reftraints of idle and artificial diftinctions. A rude mantle, which he carries conftantly about with him, ferves to defend the Arab and his family againft the oppreffive heat of the fun, as well as the inconveniencies of the rain; his robe, larger in fize, but in the ftyle of that of St. John the Baptift, woven with his own hands, which never felt the edge of the fciffars, and which he confequently owes to his own induftry alone, is all the cloathing he requires. If he looks around him, the foil, as far as he can fee, is his own, while at the fame time he affects neither land-mark nor inclofure, but fhares with his Arabian kindred the pafture of his flocks. He goes wherever he choofes, and nothing impedes his fteps; but had he been born

in

in a polifhed country, every joint of his
body would have been cramped and em-
barraffed with ligaments of twenty different
kinds, the acquifition of which would have
coft him much pain and anxiety, while
the enjoyment of them could only flat-
ter a mind of the weakeft vanity. In fine,
he would have found it difficult to turn
himfelf to the right hand or to the left,
without infringing on fome cuftom or
punctilio, equally inconfiftent, perhaps,
with the maxims of good fenfe and the
natural order of things.

That freedom and equality of condition
enjoyed by the natives, notwithftanding the
difmal afpect of their deferts, created in
my mind certain emotions of inftinctive
pleafure; an admonition which I confider
as the voice of nature, and whence I am
inclined to infer the real value and importance of thofe advantages. The circumftances of the Arab by no means preclude him from the enjoyment of pleafure;
befides an habitual and animating fenfe of
his independance, he drinks the milk of
his

his cattle, and regales himfelf with many palatable dishes to which we are ftrangers : he runs and dances with great vivacity, and practifes many other manly and ufeful exercifes. His dances are fometimes gay and exhilarating, but he is more particularly addicted to fuch as are warlike, and have a tendency to train him for the day of battle; in thefe the Arab goes through various evolutions, his lance in his hand, with the moft dextrous agility, dances equally in ufe among the Biffayan and Javanefe Indians, with this difference only, that the latter are armed with the buckler as well as the lance. The dances more peculiar to the women are of two kinds, the one fprightly and gay, the other impaffioned and voluptuous, the object of which is to excite certain ideas in a manner extremely expreffive. As in thefe it is the principal requifite that the ruling fentiment be ftrongly marked in the eye, and the expreffion of the features be in harmony with the motions and attitudes of the body, it is neceffary to the dancer's performing with approbation, that her imagination

nation be highly inflamed. Of this fpecies of dance, the Spanifh fandango, and
the calenda of America, afford a faint re-
prefentation; and it is probable the Spa-
niards, as well as the negroes of Guinea and
Angola, borrowed it from the Arabians.

Their wool, the ftaple commodity of
the deferts, ferves as the materials of cloth
and tapeftry, which for execution would by
no means difgrace the dexterity of an European manufacturer.   Of their goat-fkins
they make bottles and troughs for giving
water to their cattle. Their flocks, which,
on account of their rapid increafe, would
foon become a burthen to their owners,
they are ufed to barter in civilized countries for articles of drefs, corn, dates,
and whatever elfe their neceffities require.
Such of the Arabian tribes as border on
the Euphrates and improveable lands, cultivate a fmall portion of ground; but as
foon as the feed-time is over they betake
themfelves to the wandering purfuits of
the defert, and only return in autumn, in
order to reap the benefit of the harveft.

A tribe of Arabs on their march acrofs
the

the defert is a very extraordinary object. On
this occafion a vaft extent of plain prefents
itfelf to the eye, covered with herds and flocks,
preceded by a troop of camels laden with
tents, baggage, and poultry, animals which,
at the firft fignal for their departure, inftantly take wing and perch on the back of
the dromedary. Behind thefe is another
fet of camels, charged with all the lame
and infirm animals, which, by their various
and difcordant cries, give fufficient notice
of the pain and hardfhips of their con-
finement. Upon a third fet are groupes
of women and children, whofe painful
fcreams mix in ftrange confufion with
the bleating and bellowing of numberlefs
animals, of all humours, ages, and fpecies.
It is difficult to conceive a more irkfome fituation than that of the Arab's wife, in the
midft of her children, weeping, fighting, and
fcrambling all around her. Such of the women as are exempt from the incumbrances of
infants, employ themfelves on their camels in
fpinning, or grinding corn with hand-mills.
High above this fingular mafs of tumult
and

and diforder appears a wood of lances, at leaft eight or ten feet in length, while the ear begins to be ftunned with the hoarfe voice of the Arab, chiding, expoftulating, or commanding filence in his family, but whofe chief care is to form a ftrong rampart for the defence of the little commonwealth on its march.

It was the intention of the Bedouins to have purfued their route through the middle of the defert, which, by drawing us to a diftance from the Arabian encampments, feemed to promife fecurity againft all manner of difturbance from the natives. But it being reprefented by the Arabs of this camp, that, among other inconveniencies refulting from this ftep, we fhould not find a drop of water, either for ourfelves or camels, we determined to direct our courfe towards the banks of the Euphrates. Next day, therefore, we proceeded to lay in a ftock of water at the wells of the adjacent camp; and on this occafion I had a fecond opportunity of obferving the phlegmatic inattention of the Arab. If at any time they quitted their tents, it was not in order

to

to obferve the appearance of ftrangers, but to milk their cattle, which by the bye is the bufinefs of the women, or in the management of other domeftic concerns. We filled our bottles with the fame tranquillity as if we had been in the heart of the defert ; and I particularly remarked, that although I was the fingle individual, at this time, who was mounted on a camel, and was pointed out to their attention by fome peculiarities of drefs, I could only attract the notice of two or three little children. Some of the tribe were at the well, employed like ourfelves in filling their bottles, fome in conducting their flocks to pafture in the vicinity, and fome, after having milked their goats, called the family to breakfaft with the fame apathy and indifference as if they had been entirely by themfelves. If our prefence had any effect at all, it was upon the minds of the women, who ufed to cover a fmall part of the face upon appearing without the tent.

As foon as we were provided in water, we began our journey, keeping a little more to the N. E.; and, after travelling four days, came to a deserted castle with three towers, on the confines of a small lake. Here we were under the necessity of again filling our bottles, though the water was of a nature extremely disagreeable both to the smell and taste. Meanwhile thirst, as well as curiosity, drew me towards the castle and its lake; and I soon saw, what is an object of great rarity in those regions, a piece of water covered with bulrushes waving in the wind. It is impossible for me to describe the emotions of joy occasioned by this prospect; suffice it to say, that I approached it with all manner of alacrity; but how great was my disappointment, when, instead of the enchanting spot my imagination had suggested, I met with a piece of moist marshy ground, which contained water in all the colours of the rainbow, corrupting in the sun, and every where emitting a most pestilential odour! I made shift to penetrate to a place where it seemed to be of the greatest depth, in hopes I should find it there of a less offensive quality; but even here the water was extremely discoloured, and the

o   adjoining

adjoining reeds appearing to have acquired
its difmal hue, my ftomach revolted at the
idea of raifing it to my lips : but my tongue
was parched with the burning wind of
the defert, and appetite impelled me to
drink; fuch, however, was the fœtid tafte
of this ftagnated pool, that I was able to
gulp down one mouthful of it only; and I
retired, with little gratification either to
my thirft or curiofity. The caftle ftands
clofe to the lake, on a mound of earth
probably artificial. I made it my bufinefs
to get within the wall; but the door was
fo extremely fmall, it being only two feet
and a half high, and not more than one
half of thefe dimenfions in breadth, that I
can fcarce fuppofe it had ever been intended for common ufe. The wall was
built of earth, and of confiderable thicknefs. Having with fome difficulty made
my way into this fingular building, I found
a large fquare, in three corners of which
were three towers, whofe doors were
ftill on a fmaller fcale than the one by
which I had entered. I at length, however, got to the top, and obferved from

one

one of the towers, that, inftead of a para-
pet, the artift had inclined the wall in fuch
a manner, that one might difcover any object at the foot of the caftle.   He had likewife given the curtain between the towers
a curved form, in order, no doubt, to fa-
cilitate the means of its defence.   But
having fatisfied my curiofity as to the
nature of a building fo little expected in
the defert, I began to open my eyes to a
view of the furrounding country; and here
all my ideas of the Arabian deferts, fuch as
they may be found in the poetical language of oriental tales, were fhort of the
truth.   A ftillnefs, like the filence of night;
the faint remains of a breeze, ftill glowing
with the fervour of the meridian fun, but
now finking with his orb; around an un-
bounded wafte, covered with a dark grey
fand, refembling the afhes of a furnace, and
according with the raging heat of thofe
regions; the vaft canopy of the heavens,
acrofs whofe pale atmofphere no other object
is feen but the reddifh difk of the fun dipt
in the horizon, in the moment of his departure,—are a few of thofe interefting circumftances

cumftances which confpired, on this occafion, to imprefs my mind with an unpleaf-
ing melancholy. I defcended from the
caftle, and proceeded to join my companions.

We continued to purfue our route in the
fame direction; and in two days came to
fome wells, contiguous to four tents, the
women belonging to which gave us their
affiftance in mending and filling our bottles. Next morning I very narrowly efcaped diflocating my neck by a fall from
, my camel, as he got up to refume his
march.

In three days more we defcried, towards
evening, twelve Arabs in the defert, with
a company of camels. The chief of our
caravan, tempted, I am afraid, by the
fmallnefs of their number, having order-
ed his men to give chace, they were purfued and fired upon; and the Arabs left
behind them, in their flight, fome linen,
bottles, and clubs. I was by no means
fatisfied with this atchievement of the Bedouins; and, thinking it very improbable
that thofe men perambulated the defert

I 3   by

by themfelves, I dreaded the confequences of fo unprovoked an act of hoftility.
I compared the late extreme caution with
which I had feen our people approach the
lines of an Arabian camp, with this wanton bravado of courage againft a handful
of men entirely deftitute of arms; and fecretly condemned the conduct of the caravan.

We paffed the enfuing night, however,
without moleftation, and, early next morning, refumed our journey; but about noon,
the apprehenfions I had entertained the evening before began to be realized; for all of
a fudden we faw a body of men on horfeback, riding towards us at full fpeed. The
Bedouins ftooped their camels, and entered into a conference with a meffenger who
came to treat with us on the part of the
enemy. It was but too evident, however,
they could come to no agreement; for the
Arab returned to his friends, and our caravan ran inftantly to arms.

Meanwhile we continued our march;
but, after an interval of little more than a
quarter of an hour, we obferved a large
body

body of horfe and foot in purfuit of
us. We again ftooped our camels as
compactly as poffible, at the fame time
difplaying a flag, containing certain figures and characters in white upon a
blue ground. Our mufketeers, advancing
about two hundred paces, pofted themfelves in the front of the caravan. The
lances halted at the diftance of fifty
paces before the Bedouin ftandard, which
was erected at the corner of the camp,
on the fide of the enemy, and defended by
the reft of the Bedouins, armed chiefly
with clubs and fabres. The Arabs advanced in order of battle, to the number
of five hundred men, while our whole
force confifted only of a hundred and
fifty. The Bedouins, however, waited
their approach with fteadinefs and refolution, fhouting " Allah-ou-Allah!" which
I underftood to be an invocation of
God to witnefs the juftice of their caufe,
and to fuccour them in battle. The
enemy having approached within the diftance of two hundred paces from our mufketeers, began a kind of running fight,

I 4   fuch

fuch as I had feen practifed in the Arabian camp, which I have already had frequent occafions to mention. The Bedouins kept up an irregular fire upon their opponents; when the Arabs, extending themfelves as if they had meant to furround us, chofe to decline a clofe engagement, and were contented with difcharging their pieces againft the caravan. When at any time, however, they feemed defirous of clofing with the Bedouins, we rofe in a body, and advanced full fpeed to meet them; while they, as it would feem, perceiving we were prepared for the conflict, retreated flowly on the plain.

The engagement continued to be maintained in this indecifive manner, till the approach of night, when the main body of the enemy having retired a confiderable diftance from the caravan, the mufketeers drew nearer to each other. On our fide there was not one man killed or wounded, while the Bedouins boafted of having killed three or four men and two camels belonging to the Arabs. We kept, during the night, a picquet towards

wards the enemy, as well as a rear-guard, which was more immediately charged with the fafety of the caravan. The clofe attention given by both parties to the fignal or watch-word, which was repeated in very extraordinary cries, fuggefted no mean idea of their military conduct and circumfpection. Now all was joy and uproar in the Bedouin camp; and our warriors, elated with the fuccefs of the preceding day, celebrated the triumph of victory by dances defcriptive of all the manœuvres of an Arabian battle. At the fame time, while it was their bufinefs to ftimulate the national courage of the tribe, by the frequent repetition of " Ben Halet," they were equally anxious to excite their whole rage againft their opponents, by the moft violent exclamations of " Turkis," or "Turk," which fignifies, in their acceptation of the word, an implacable enemy. I took the liberty of obferving to my conductor, who feemed to be a fenfible as well as brave man, that a little repofe would, in my opinion, be a better preparative for a new engagement in the morning, than thofe
intemperate

intemperate and unfeafonable gufts of
joy; and likewife, that, without waiting
till the Arabs fhould be ftrengthened by
the arrival of any additional force, we
ought to refume our march by day-break,
placing our camels in the center, and our
armed men on the two wings, who might
be in conftant readinefs to repel the attacks
of the enemy. My advice was little regarded, and I was not fufficiently acquainted with the Arabic language to deliver my opinion in a council of war,
which was now fitting round the Bedouin ftandard. I committed myfelf, therefore, to the wifdom of Providence, and refolved to profit by a fmall interval of repofe, which, however, was liable to be
interrupted by the balls of the Arabs, which
at times whiftled about my ears.

The engagement was renewed early
in the morning; and, after lafting two
hours, fimilar in all refpects to that
of the preceding day, the combatants
on both fides withdrew from the field.
The caravan had a fecond conference
with the enemy; and at eight o'clock
I received

I received a meſſage from the Bedouins,
deſiring me to deliver them all the money in my poſſeſſion; to which requi-
ſition I very readily conſented. Couriers,
however, were continually arriving as before, and, as I heard no farther mention of
the money, probably intended for our ran-
ſom, I concluded that all notion of recon-
cilement between the contending parties
was at an end : accordingly I ſoon learned, that the enemy would accept of nothing
leſs than the plunder of the whole caravan,
and that, to complete this unfortunate adventure, we were now wholly at their diſcretion. I am convinced, however, that ſo
great an animoſity to the caravan, who, according to cuſtom immemorial, is conſtantly
permitted, for a certain acknowledgment in
money, to proceed without diſturbance, could
only be owing to our wanton attack of the
twelve Arabs, aggravated, perhaps, by ſome
effuſion of blood in the firſt engagement.
Upon receiving a final anſwer from the
enemy, we again ſtood to our arms, though
conſcious we were far from being in a condition to hold out for any length of time
against

againſt the hardſhips of our preſent ſituation. It was now five days ſince we laſt
filled our bottles, and our water was nearly
exhauſted. Beſides, the exceſſive heat
and the conſtant fatigue and agitation of
body and mind, to which we had for a
conſiderable time been expoſed, had intirely exhauſted our ſtrength.

Towards evening the Arabs made a feint
to renew the attack, but they declined approaching nearer than the diſtance of a gun-
ſhot, and we had not one man either killed
or wounded. Night coming on, the enemy
retired to the diſtance of half a league on
the plain; when we took care, as before, to
place an advanced guard, which, with ſen-
tinels ſtationed on all ſides of the caravan,
watched the motions of the enemy. Having obſerved that our men, after lighting a
great many fires in the camp, formed themſelves into ſmall circles, and whiſpered each
other in the ear, I began to conjecture that
ſome ſudden and ſecret enterprize was in
agitation: accordingly, about ten o'clock
they began to ſaddle their camels, and my
conductor deſired me to give him my
linen,

linen, that he might pack it up with his own. Another Bedouin, having charged himfelf with the leaft weighty part of my pro- vifions, advifed me to abandon the re- mainder. I faw the whole caravan em- ployed in a fimilar manner; and, every thing being concerted and ready, I was exhorted to be on my guard, and above all things to ftick faft to my dromedary, for that in a few moments the caravan would betake itfelf to flight.

What a difmal profpect was now before me! I was to follow the caravan at the dreadful gallop of the camel; the hard ftep and ftubborn nature of which muft expofe me every inftant to the moft alarming ac- cidents. If unfortunately I fhould happen to fall at the firft outfet, I muft either be crufhed to death by my companions, or be left alone a prey to all the miferies of the defert. In this cafe my only chance of fafety would have been, by purfuing a northern courfe to have endeavoured to reach the banks of the Euphrates, which at this fea- fon are frequented by Arabian tribes; but which were diftant at leaft four days journey.

There

There were moments when I could not help fecretly wifhing the enemy to overtake us, being fatisfied I had now nothing more defirable to expect, than either to perifh by the fword, or to furrender myfelf a prifoner. But I had been told the Arabs are accuftomed to give no quarter to their enemies, even after plundering them of their goods, confidering themfelves bound by the ties of hofpitality only within the lines of their tents, which were probably at a great diftance. I refigned myfelf, therefore, to the difpofal of Divine Providence, and, having placed myfelf firm on my bolfters, expected patiently the fignal for flight.

About four o'clock in the morning they fet up the ufual cry, *Bonne garde?* or, Who goes there? while at the fame time the Bedouins were bufily employed, all over the camp, in lighting up fires, which, as they were only kept alive by a fort of withered bramble gleaned in the defert, were of very fhort duration. This ftratagem was fucceeded by an interval of dead filence; but at half an hour after four, as the

the advanced guard was ſtill hollowing
Bonne garde? my good Arab came to ſee if
I was properly ſeated on my camel, and in
the ſame inſtant the whole caravan ſhot
over the deſert like a flaſh of lightning
into the S. W.

Acroſs an amazing cloud of duſt, occaſioned by the abrupt manner of our departure, and which muſt have been ter-
rible to a ſpectator at a diſtance, I began
to obſerve that the young camels, intended
for ſale, had each a fetter on one of his
feet; a precaution which was meant to
free us of their incumbrance, as well as to
obſtruct the progreſs of the Arabs, by di-
verting their attention from the great object of their purſuit. We fled three leagues
towards the ſouth, at the full ſtretch of the
dromedary; in the courſe of which I ſat
perched as upon a table; and nothing but
the hand of Providence could have pre-
vented my falling from the back of this
animal, whoſe motions were ſo intolerably
ſevere, that at every ſtep my bowels ſeemed
to be ſhaken in pieces. My hands, one
holding faſt before and the other behind,

ſupported

supported me like a kind of buttress, by which means they were already much bruised and lacerated, while my nerves had loft their spring and sensibility in so great a degree, that I was twenty times on the point of abandoning my hold.

Meanwhile the enemy were in close pursuit of us; but a part of our caravan having fallen into their hands, they loft some time in pillaging their effects and catching the young camels; and on this occasion my poor Arabian cook, whom I hired at Baffora, had the misfortune to be in the number of the captives. The enemy, however, being occupied with their plunder, gave us time to leave them considerably behind; and therefore, after running three leagues further S. E. our little troop, which by this time confifted of seven persons only, resolved to detach ourselves intirely from the remains of the caravan. What was the fate of the other Arabs, I cannot pretend to say, having never, from that moment, received the smalleft intelligence concerning them. We now made a large circuit round the region we had juft traverfed,

traverfed, and thus, by leaving our pur-
fuers, and the reft of the caravan, to profecute a route directly contrary to ours, we
refumed our former direction towards the
N. W.

Having continued our flight in this
quarter with the fame celerity, we at length
came to a diftrict of the defert covered
with large ftones and fragments of rocks;
and here my camel ftumbling againft a
ftone, and at the fame inftant making a
jerk to one fide of the path, I loft my
hold, and was thrown off to fome diftance;
but happily a good Arab was at hand, who
immediately ftooped his camel, and took
me up behind him; my dromedary, mean
time, having taken flight, overturned his
baggage, and a Bedouin cutting the ropes, I
was deprived at once of all my provifions,
with a confiderable part of my other neceffaries, while my camel marched un-
loaded before us.

About eight o'clock we entered the dry
bed of a torrent, and were at pains to
conceal ourfelves, whilft one of our men

Vol. II.   K   went

went to reconnoitre from an eminence what was paffing in the plain. He could difcover neither the enemy nor the caravan, and we again mounted our camels; but I was now feated on a miferable pack-faddle, confifting of a rude bolfter of hay placed round the dromedary's bunch, with four pieces of a board imitating the ftock of a faddle; and as we purfued our route nearly with the fame difpatch as we had done before, my fufferings are not to be defcribed.

At ten, in the vicinity of a rock, we difcovered a fpring of fweet water furrounded with fhrubs, a circumftance which feemed to announce it of a good quality. Being now completely worn out with thirft and fatigue, I was unable to reftrain the importunity of nature, and took almoft a bottle of it at one draught; but I foon became indifpofed, and had reafon to be forry for the imprudence of my conduct. If we had had any fufpicion of meeting the enemy in this quarter, the recent traces of cattle which had been watering in the morning muft have increafed our apprehenfions. We took care, however, to place

o   a fentinel

a fentinel on a rifing ground, who kept a
fharp look-out, while we remained in readinefs to continue our flight at the firft
fignal. As he could difcover neither man
nor beaft in the wide extent of the defert,
we began to be fatisfied that our counter-
march had entirely efcaped the obfervation
of the Arabs.

I now confidered in what manner I
could reward my friend the Arab, who
fo generoufly ftooped his dromedary, and
took me up behind him, when I had the
misfortune to fall from my own. I could
not fail to reflect that while he delivered
me from immediate death, or perhaps from
the more deplorable calamity of ftarving
in the defert, he had expofed himfelf to
the imminent danger of falling into the
hands of an enraged enemy. My money
was reduced to the very trifling fum of
four piaftres, which, with an earneft requeft that he would accept of them as
a fmall teftimony of affectionate gratitude,
I prefented to my benefactor. So familiar, however, are the fentiments of charity
and beneficence to the minds of thofe peo-

ple,

ple, that he had no idea of what prompted me to offer him money. Upon his modeſt but peremptory refuſal, I laid the pieces on his robe, and left him; but in a few minutes he came to me with the money in his hand; and ſuch was the extreme delicacy of this worthy man's feelings, that he was not perſuaded into compliance, until I had aſſured him that I offered theſe piaſtres, not as the reward of his ſervices, but as the memorial of a friend, who loved and eſteemed him.

I had now no proviſions of my own, having loſt them in the deſert; but I had little cauſe of regret, as the good Arabs took care to adminiſter to my wants. They baked oaten cakes, and toaſted them on the ſand, or at a fire of brambles, and having ſpread them with dates, or butter obtained from the milk of the female camel, applied them a ſecond time to the heat. At our meals I was conſtantly treated with a larger portion of this buttered cake, which is far from being a bad kind of ragout, than fell to the ſhare of any one of my companions; by reaſon, however, of the

great

great diminution of provifions, it was but feldom we could afford this treat, and were obliged to have recourfe to dates as our chief means of fubfiftence. This fingular attention in the Bedouins to my fupport, which was above the fufpicion of an interefted motive, continued to be exercifed in the fame manner and degree to the day of our feparation.

Our fears of the enemy, which were greatly encreafed by frefh traces of cattle vifible about the well, not permitting us to linger, after dinner we mounted our camels, and fled till night, almoft with the fame rapidity as in the morning. My pain and fatigue were fcarce to be borne; every inch of my feat applied to the pack-faddle was covered with fores, and, partly owing to my infirmities, and partly to the loofe condition of the faddle, which was thrown backwards at every ftep of the dromedary, I was frequently pitched upon his hump. My nerves were benumbed, and become incapable of farther exertions, while my fingers, in confequence of an extreme

agitation

agitation in my blood, fhaked involuntarily, like the keys of a harpfichord. In this miferable condition, having loft my appetite, I was unable to take what nourifhment was neceffary for my fupport; but I looked forward with hope of relief to that refrefhing repofe I promifed myfelf in the approaching night. About nine o'clock in the evening, however, I was told by the Arabs that it was neceffary to go on. There was no time left to expoftulate; I mounted my dromedary in the beft manner I was able, and went on at a long ftep, which I endeavoured to bear with all the patience in my power.

At two o'clock in the morning we halted at a piece of hollow ground, where we lay down and flept till fix. Mounting our camels again, we purfued our journey the whole day, fometimes at a trot, fometimes at a kind of gallop, according as the defert feemed more or lefs frequented. The following morning we difcovered the banks of the Euphrates, on which ftood a folitary building; but having fuddenly obferved a
company

company of Arabs, we turned the heads of
our camels, and fled full fpeed. We paffed
heaps of ftones at different intervals, which
were probably defigned for a direction of
the road. I obferved likewife large mounds
of earth, but whether natural or artificial
I cannot pretend to fay. In regulating
our flight, we were directed by the N. W.
wind in the day-time, and at night took
our direction from the motions of the
ftars.

The dromedary here, which differs from
that of Africa, being fmaller, and having
but one bunch, feems to be particularly
intended for the ufe of man in thofe defert
regions. Notwithftanding the extreme
fatigue to which he was fubjected in confequence of very long ftages, and although
he was occafionally four or five days without water, eating only a few brambles,
which he gleaned in the defert in the
hurry of his march, he appeared to have
no manner of complaint. Befides, he remained ftooped, according to cuftom, during the whole courfe of the night; but he

is

is endowed with the faculty of bringing
up his food, which he fwallows at firft in
hafte, and which he ruminates afterwards
at his convenience, in the manner of the
ox. It is unneceffary for me to defcribe
the ftructure of an animal which is fo univerfally known.

Our difcovery at this moment of a
well was a fortunate event, as our bottles
were almoft entirely empty; but, finding
it expedient to fpend little time in taking
our fupply of water, we departed as we had
arrived, at full fpeed, in order to elude the
keepers of cattle, whofe traces were obfervable all around it.

In four days we faw a ridge of high
mountains on the left, ftretching along
the horizon; and a little afterwards there
appeared a fmall cloud, followed by feveral
others, which, as the defert had hitherto
prefented a fky uniformly ferene, was become an object of fome curiofity.

We were ftill, however, fubjected to
unremitting anxiety and fatigue, from
marches and counter-marches, which we
were obliged to make as often as we
difcovered

difcovered the traces of a camel, or the footfteps of an Arab. As the little bottoms in the defert are much frequented by the natives in the fummer feafon, it often happened that, in order to avoid being difcovered after reaching the top of an eminence, we found it expedient to turn, and defcend it at full fpeed. When, which was often the cafe, our march happened to lie through a narrow and difficult paffage, we made it our bufinefs to hide ourfelves during the day, and refumed our journey at the approach of night.

We now began to draw near to the high mountains above mentioned, when I obferved the little vallies of their vicinity white with falt-petre, which had no doubt been depofited by the winter rains. In fome places the foil, formed into a dry cruft, was raifed about four inches above the level of the folid ground; infomuch that our camels, under whofe feet it broke at every ftep, found it extremely difficult to proceed. This uncommon puffed ftate of the foil is evidently occafioned by the

exceffive

exceffive heat of the fun, which fets in at the end of the rainy feafon.

My fellow-travellers were at pains to direct my eye to a town fituated among thofe mountains, whofe name I have forgotten, and which I was unable to perceive. I faw an Arabian fair in the plain, and paffed fome ancient ruins, which, however, from their fize, did not feem to merit much of the traveller's attention.

We met with the veftiges of encampments, which, in the winter feafon, the Arab pitches upon the heights, and generally in the vicinity of a torrent. Here the foil is of greater depth, but, on account of numberlefs rat-holes, which are probably abandoned as foon as the drought commences, is extremely painful to the feet of the camel: the earth being completely undermined, the moment he fets his foot on the ground, the cruft gives way, and it is not without a confiderable effort that he can extricate his hoof from the foil. Happily, however, in this embarraffing fituation we were not under the

necefity

neceffity of travelling with our ufual expedition.

We turned to the right, and, directing
our march in the line of the mountains,
arrived at a watering-place in the midft of
a plain. Having here defcended into a
very deep cavern, formed by huge rocks,
we found in a vaft bafon or cavity a fountain of bitter water, which, confidering its
tafte, fmell, colour, and fituation, merits
a place in the catalogue of the infernal
fources. Next day, at fome diftance from
this cave, we lay concealed in the hollows,
and as foon as it was dark refumed our
journey along the fide of the hills. We
had the benefit of the moon till ten, when
we ftopped, and waited her going down;
for, as we were about to enter a long and
narrow defile, in order that we might be
more in the direction of Aleppo, we were
afraid of falling in with the natives. Having lately feen an Arabian fair in the plain,
and as we had obferved in the courfe of
the day that this confined paffage, as well
as the adjacent grounds, were frequented
by Arabs, the apprehenfions of my fellow-
travellers

travellers were far from appearing extra-
vagant. We fent a fcout before, to reconnoitre, and ftole on without uttering
a fingle word; for, from the dead ftillnefs which reigns over the face of the
defert, a very fmall noife may be heard
at a confiderable diftance. Even our camels, whofe inftincts are truly wonder-
ful, feemed to conduct themfelves under
fimilar impreffions. At midnight I heard
the found of a bell in the defert, and foon
after obferved fome Arabs of a neighbouring camp, who were leading an afs. Dreading the confequences of being difcovered,
we lay down behind our camels, not without apprehending, however, that the noife
of the Arabs might put our animals to
flight. Fortunately they remained quiet,
and our fcout returned in a little time
from taking a view of the country; but as
we were in a ftate of uncertainty whether
we had not been difcovered by the Arabs
who had juft paffed us, and as it was the
opinion of our fpy, that it would be extremely dangerous to hazard the paffage under the prefent circumftances, we mounted

our

our camels in profound filence, and betook
ourfelves to flight.

Continuing our route in the line of the
fame mountains, we began to afcend them
the next day ; but we had no fooner reached the top of the firft ridge, than, looking
back upon the plain, we faw it crouded
with Arabian camps, and could not help
congratulating ourfelves on our fortunate
efcape. Thefe are the firft heights of any
confequence which we had met with fince
our departure from Baffora. Here the foil
begins to be a little more fufceptible of cul-
ture, and the brambles feem of a different fpecies from thofe of the defert.
We faw a wild-boar turn into the recefs
of a mountain. Upon defcending we entered a vaft plain, with diftant hills on each
fide of us. Our profpects had now loft a
great deal of their former dreary uniformity.
Although I was in fome degree recovered
from my firft fatigue, and a little more accuftomed to my fituation, the rude motion
of the dromedary proved ftill extremely
painful. I cannot impute my bad condition, however, to any particular delicacy

of

of conftitution, fince one of the hardy Bedouins frequently lagged behind, and appeared at leaft to be equally worn out with myfelf.   In our flight over the defert I laboured under one great and peculiar difadvantage, I mean my inability to keep the camel to his proper pace; for thofe who are ufed to travel on this animal feldom go at a trot, but almoft always at a kind of amble, which is equally expeditious, and much lefs fevere to the rider. As this animal is actuated by a furprifing emulation to pafs his companions on the road, when I happened to have the misfortune to be left behind, his impatience to come up with them made him conftantly fall into a moft formidable trot, which it was by no means in my power either to moderate or prevent.

We filled our bottles at a well of excellent water, fituated in a kind of yard, and furrounded by the ruins of a confiderable caftle; but obferving the ground ftill moift with water that had been recently drawn, we thought it advifeable to fpend but little

time

time in this place. We continued our journey, with the mountains always on the right, fleeping ftill in the hollows during night. Next day we travelled in the fame direction, permitting our camels to graze at intervals among the rocks which cover-ed us from the obfervation of the natives. At night we proceeded along a path formed in the channel of a torrent, but quitted it in the morning to purfue our march in the direction of the mountains.

Here the footfteps of the camel become very obfervable, while the defert begins to be beaten, and to have the appearance of being much more frequented than former-ly. Even in this place we were obliged to pafs the day as ufual, fkulking in the dry bed of a torrent, and continuing our journey during the night by the foot of the mountains.

At eight o'clock I obferved a fire on the heights, and heard the barking of dogs, which had probably perceived us in the de-fert; fymptoms of population, which were foon confirmed by evident veftiges of the plough. At twelve we croffed feveral

cultivated

cultivated fields, feparated from one another by fmall ditches. At one o'clock in
the morning we came to houfes, and a
brook of running water, for the firft time
fince we left the confines of Baffora; and
having at length entered a built village, we
ftooped our dromedaries, and ftood to our
arms. Every foul in the village feemed
to be afleep, and I was not a little inclined
to follow their example.

The return of day prefented us with a
country watered with the rain and dew of
heaven, and in no mean ftate of improve-
ment; upon which ftood a number of pop-
lars, the firft tree I obferved after fetting
foot on the defert. The villagers, inti-
midated by our warlike appearance, and
probably miftaking us for a band of robbers who had lately committed depredations in the wildernefs, came to requeft
that we would withdraw into an adjacent
field, where we fhould be at liberty to
refrefh ourfelves unmolefted. We fub-
mitted; and, having refted till eleven,
we again mounted our camels, and continued our journey in the direction of a
country

country which appeared ftill more beautiful and populous.

Meanwhile I was much entertained with
the great confternation which a moft complete change in the appearance of furrounding objects produced in our camels. The
different afpect of a Turk and an Arab in
drefs, figure, and ftature; the novelty of
houfes, dogs, trees, and rivulets; in fhort,
every thing occurred in its turn as a caufe of
difmay; a circumftance which was attended with frefh difficulties to the traveller,
though of a very different nature from
thofe he had lately experienced. Our animals continued to advance with unabating
diffidence and trepidation ; and, on one occafion, a rat happening to run acrofs the
road, threw our whole troop into great terror and confufion. One of our men was
difmounted, and it was not without much
difficulty that the reft of the company were
able to keep their feats. At the entrance
to the firft bridge, the dromedary, apprehending, perhaps from the found of his
foot-fteps, there was fome want of folidity
below, made a dead paufe; and a con-

fiderable fpace of time paffed before we could accomplifh our paffage.

We paffed frequent villages, and were now travelling through a country like one continued garden, producing trees and plants of various kinds. At four in the afternoon we came to a kind of arcade, within which was a charming fountain of water ; but the Bedouins, being feized with the difquietude and hefitation of their camels, ftopped fhort, and declined to enter it, until one of their number had reconnoitred the place. Paffing feveral watermills, and a burying-ground, we at laft perceived, at fome diftance before us, the walls of a great town. The numbers of the dead obfervable in the multitude of grave-ftones, the rich appearance of the adjacent country, and many fine gardens along the road, fuggefted the idea of a very extenfive city. After proceeding a confiderable way on the outfide of the townwall, we were about to halt for refrefhment, when we received a meffage from the bafha, ordering us inftantly to depart ; at the fame time threatening us with the whole

whole weight of his difpleafure in cafe of difobedience. Senfible that we were at the mercy of a tyrant, we thought it expedient to withdraw to fome diftance; but we foon received a fimilar notice, and I began to imagine that the terror of the inhabitants, at the approach of armed Bedouins, is fo great that every one trembles for his own fecurity as long as they remain in his neighbourhood. Meanwhile a bold Arab, highly incenfed at the infolence of the people, and whofe patience was unable to brook any farther interruption, ftooped his dromedary, and planted his lance in the ground, in order to denote his right of poffeffion; and in fpite of the reproaches and violent abufe poured upon us from the furrounding gardens, the whole band inftantly followed his example. On the third of Auguft, therefore, and on the thirty-fifth day fince our departure from Baffora, we fixed our quarters in the vicinity of this city.

Our marches and counter-marches in the defert had occafioned fuch confufion in my ideas, refpecting the direction of our

route, that I now found it extremely difficult to determine by the maps the place
of our prefent encampment.   Having obferved that the general line of our march
was greatly to the W. of Aleppo, I could
find nothing in my geographical computa-
tions, at our fuppofed diftance from the
fea, that could at all correfpond to it, but
the ancient city of Damafcus.   I afked my
companions if this was not the name of
the town; but was anfwered, that it was
called *Chams*, or the City of the Sun; that
it was governed by a very powerful bafha;
and that the name of my country had never
yet reached the ears of the inhabitants.   It
was added, that the people are a peculiarly vicious and malevolent race; and indeed
I was not mifinformed, if I may depend
for proof on thofe horrid curfes and exe-
crations regularly poured out againft the
Turks, as often as the Bedouins returned
from market.   Refpecting our actual fituation on the globe, however, I was now more
in the dark than before; and, being told
that Aleppo was ftill at the diftance of ten
days journey, I urged my conductor to fet

out

out with me foon for that place. In the
mean time I was faint with hunger and fatigue, and therefore fent immediately to
Chams for provifions, which we devoured
with great eagernefs the moment they were
fet before us. I bathed to refrefh my weary
limbs, changed my drefs, and made it my
bufinefs to profit by the prefent interval of
repofe.

I now entreated my conductor to lead
me to fome inn or houfe of entertainment for ftrangers; but, to a man whofe
notions and habits of life were fo little
familiar to European manners, my pro-
pofal plainly appeared idle and ridiculous. Befides, he was under no fmall
concern, left I fhould be molefted, and
even infulted by the Turks. Next day,
having expreffed my defire of making
fome acquaintance with the Afiatic
Chriftians, it was not long till he introduced me to a man of the Syriac
ritual, from whom I learned, that Chams
is the name the Arabs give to Damafcus.
Afterwards I met with a father jefuit in the
ftreets, dreffed in the fafhion of the coun-

try,

try, who, upon hearing I was French, aſſured me he was of the ſame nation, and invited me to an aſylum in his *hoſpice* or convent; a favour which I accepted with much pleaſure and alacrity.

The city of Damaſcus is large and populous. The houſes in front, or on the ſide of the ſtreet, are very indifferent; but they preſent a handſome appearance towards the gardens. It contains manufactures in various branches; the marketplaces are well conſtructed, and ornamented with a rich colonade of variegated marble. The ſtreets, in general, are tolerably broad; but the diſtrict frequented by Chriſtians is mean, and in all reſpects much inferior to the other quarters of the town.

The great trade and population of Damaſcus, as well as the high veneration in which it is held by Muſſulmen, are owing to its being the place of general rendezvous for the Mahometan pilgrims of Europe, and the northern parts of Syria, on their way to Mecca, a circumſtance which has entitled it Mahomet's Heel.

The caravan of Mecca is always conducted

ducted by the basha of Damascus, who
receives a confiderable appointment from
the Porte on this account, as well as to
maintain a military force, and to keep certain castles on the desert in repair. These
forts are to defend the pilgrim wells against
the ravages of the Arabs, who are regularly paid a certain tribute by the caravan
for liberty to pass unmolested. They are
joined, at a certain distance from Damafcus, by the caravans of Bagdad and Grand
Cairo; in the first of which are pilgrims
from all the fouthern parts of Asia, and in
the latter similar followers of their prophet
from the different tribes and nations of
Africa. As the caravan's arrival at Mecca
is fixed for the two great folemnities, the
feast of Courban Beyran, or Abraham's facrifice, and that of Beyran, or the Turkish
carnival, at the end of Ramadan, and correfponding to the Jewish paffover, it must
not be detained at Damafcus beyond the
ordinary period of its departure, under any
pretext whatever.

The jefuits of Damafcus shewed me
every attention and civility in their power;

and

and indeed the hofpitality they afforded me
in a city which properly does not contain one
refident European, and where the manners
of the people are uncommonly cruel and
ferocious, was the moft grateful and feafonable of all the inftances of kindnefs I
received in the whole courfe of my travels.   In fine, the good fathers found
me a guide to *Baruth,* on the borders
of the Mediterranean, four days journey
from Damafcus; and therefore, after
paffing near a week in their *hofpice,* I
bade adieu to my friends the jefuits.

CHAP. V.

Travels from Damascus to Baruth, Sidon,
and St. John d'Acre; with different ex-
cursions to Mount Lebanon, the coun-
try of the Quesrouan, and that of the
Druses.

HAVING set out from Damascus for Baruth, with the mountains as formerly on the right, a tolerable road led us to their summit; and at ten o'clock, after eight hours march, put up at a small village. Though the soil is extremely dry, with little appearance of cultivation, I found here excellent fruit, milk, and vegetables. Resuming our journey in the course of the night, after ascending and descending for a considerable time, we entered a narrow defile of great length, which introduced us to a large and exten-five plain named Beca, somewhat marshy, but of a black and fertile soil. Near to the centre of this plain we crossed a small

river,

river, and foon came to a village, which ferves as a granary for the greateft part of the grain raifed in the neighbouring parts of the country. We left this village at our ufual hour of the night, and afcended high and craggy mountains, which, however, were cultivated as much as appeared compatible with the nature and quality of the foil: the difficulty and fatigue of afcending and defcending them are fo great, that feveral of our mules fell lame, and we were obliged to continue our progrefs on foot.

As every inch of the little foil the natives owe to nature is planted with vineyards, mulberries, and fruit-trees, we were well fupplied upon the road with fruits of various kinds, which grow in abundance amongft thefe wild and difmal rocks. We ftopped at a cottage in order to take fome refrefhment, where I obferved the remains of a confiderable fountain, which formerly ufed to water the mulberry-trees in its vicinity.

The Afiatic method of cultivating the mulberry is different from that in ufe
among

among Europeans. According to the latter, though at a certain feafon the tree is deprived of its leaves, ftill it is permitted to rife to its full growth; whereas, by the former, at the fame time that it is ftripped of its leaves it is lopped of its branches; and hence the mulberry-tree of eaftern countries is feldom above eight or nine feet high.

In this country I was every where hofpitably received. The common food of the inhabitants confifts of fweet and four milk, and a fort of crape-cakes toafted on a cylinder of hewn ftone, which is heated from within. The milk of this country I found much better than that of the defert, which was not only four, but hardened to the confiftency of a flint ftone.

The natives of the mountains have a noble fimplicity of character, equally removed from the domineering arrogance of the Turk, and that mean fervility of fpirit, which, I am forry to fay, feems to debafe the Chriftian vifage within the walls of Damafcus. The Chriftians of that city,

partly

partly owing to Mahometan tyranny, and partly to their own daftardly behaviour, are fubjected to the condition, and merit the appellation, of flaves, rather than the character of men.

We proceeded on our journey during night, though at the fhort diftance of five or fix leagues from Baruth; and having arrived at the top of the mountains, I at laft came in view of the Mediterranean, when I gave thanks to the Almighty for having conducted me to the profpect of thofe waters which wafh the fhores of my native country. The fky was heavily overcaft, and we had the firft fhower of rain I had met with in thofe climates, while the regions of the atmofphere, fraught with vaft maffes of vapour, towering with magnificence, in various forms and to different elevations, prefented an appearance which was far from being familiar to my late experience. On the frigid fummits of thofe mountains, however, I could not help feeling fome regret for the warmer climates I was leaving behind me.

In our gradual defcent from the heights

✝   we

we came in fight of an extenfive plain, whofe lively verdure was fingularly grateful to the eye. Here the fprings pouring down from the ridges gently water or entirely overflow the fkirts of the mountains; and hence the charming green of thofe little patches of good ground which are found interfperfed among the rocks. The fprings uniting their ftreams in their progrefs towards the bottom of the mountain, form little noify torrents, which again diverging into various channels, after wafhing the roots of the hills, proceed to moiften and fertilize the adjacent plain. We came to a little fort or caftle, fituated on a fmall river, which being above the level of a great extent of mulberries, waters them with all the advantage of the moft feafonable and fertilizing fhowers. Through thefe plantations we profecuted our journey, where the foil is fo highly cultivated that it was difficult to difcover a fingle foot of wafte or fallow ground; water, however, becomes more fcarce, in proportion as the traveller removes from the foot of the mountains. We now came in view of Baruth,

where

where we arrived with eafe at nine in the morning. I alighted at the cuftom-houfe, whence, after feeing my things examined, I went to a convent of Capuchin friars, where the good fathers gave me a kind and hofpitable reception.

I had a letter from the jefuits of Damafcus to the fuperior of a convent of that order in the Quefrouan, a diftrict of Lebanon inhabited only by the Maronites, whom I was defirous to vifit. I received all the information I wanted from the fuperior of this convent, whofe placid but animated countenance was an index to the delicacy and fenfibility of his mind, as well as to that pure and unaffected zeal by which he is actuated in the functions of his miffion. I paffed only two days in this town, which is inconfiderable in fize, and miferably built. Baruth, as well as a great part of the neighbouring mountains, are under the jurifdiction of an emir, who is tributary to the Turks; a circumftance to which the people owe their freedom from Ottoman oppreffion. In this city Chriftians and Mahometans live on friendly terms, partly owing to

the

the rigour of public juftice, which is adminiftered with great impartiality, and
partly to that prompt vengeance which is
generally inflicted on the fpot by the
party aggrieved.

I now departed for the Quefrouan, after
hearing it much extolled for its natural
ftrength, a felicity it owes to thofe lofty
mountains with which it is furrounded,
as well as to the population and native
valour of the people. I had likewife heard
that I fhould find there many convents for
the ufe of both fexes; that the rites of the
Romifh religion are as freely exercifed in
the Quefrouan as in any province of
France; and, in a word, that thofe mountaineers grant toleration to no other religious fect whatever.

With thefe and fimilar impreffions on
my mind, I paffed a little river in the
plains of Baruth, and continuing my journey by the fea fhore on the road to Tripoli,
I came to the foot of a mountain, which
is only to be afcended by flights of fteps
cut in the folid rock. This is one of thofe
great works which continue to preferve
the

the memory of the Romans, many of
whofe infcriptions on this road ftill meet
the eye of the traveller. All along the path,
which is about twelve feet broad, they had
ufed the precaution to make holes correfponding to the hoofs of their horfes, in
order to prevent them from flipping or
falling on the ftones. Rails have been very
properly extended on the fide next the
fea, which heaves its billows with great
violence, and to a great height, againft
the rocks, whilft towards land the head
of the traveller becomes giddy as he looks
down the frightful precipice.

Having afcended this extraordinary path,
which is by no means difficult, and defcended in the fame manner on the oppofite
fide, I paffed what is called Dog's River,
at two leagues diftance from Baruth.   On
the border of the fea I obferved a diftrict
of mulberries, which receive their neceffary fupplies of moifture from that river,
by means of various canals.   Having no
occafion to pafs that way, I ftruck off to
the right, and afcending the banks of the
river, which at firft are much confined by

fteep

steep rocks, but afterwards open into a little valley planted with mulberries, I came on the left to a mountain, gradually rising into the form of an amphitheatre, and planted with different species of timber. I forded Dog's river above a considerable bridge, on which I found an inscription, and ascending by a path extremely steep and difficult, I at last reached the top of the mountain, and paid my respects to a Maronitic convent named Louisey, whose church is tolerably neat and clean; thence I discovered on a hill the jesuits hospice of Aintoura, to which I was directed, and in my way towards it passed a populous village. I crossed a narrow valley, which, though the soil is watered with few springs, and consequently less fertile than the lower grounds, is covered, like all others in this country, with fig-trees, mulberries, and vineyards. Pursuing a gradual ascent along-side of the mountain, I left a little to the right a large village standing on a fine champain country in good cultivation, and after travelling about a league further on the same

VOL. II. M ridge,

ridge, I faw on a little eminence before me a convent of nuns, who are under the infpection of the jefuits; and at laft arrived at the hofpice of Aintoura, fituated two leagues from the river of Dogs.

I was well received by the fuperior, delivered him a letter from Damafcus, and expreffed an earneft defire of vifiting the Quefrouan; he engaged to afford me every means in his power of gratifying my wifhes. This religious houfe is fituated at a third of the whole height from the top of a mountain, which, though extremely fteep and difficult of afcent, is cultivated and planted to the very fummit; the foil is particularly dry and ftony, and yet the trees and vines appear frefh and every way in good condition. The houfes are not collected in the manner of villages, but thinly fcattered all over the mountain. Befides the convent of nuns above mentioned, there is higher on the mountain a feminary, in which the jefuits educate a number of young men deftined to the fervice of the altar. The ftudents were at this time

greatly

greatly incumbered by a princefs, widow
of a certain emir, who, upon her embrac-
ing the Romifh religion, had requefted
permiffion to refide for fome time in the feminary.

By means of the fuperior I became acquainted with a cheik or lord of the country, who lives at two leagues diftance, in
a village named Jelton. The greateft part
of the Chriftian cheiks related to the reigning family, which is very numerous, and
divided into different branches, refide in
this village. The third day of my vifit to
the Quefrouan jefuits, the fuperior gave
me a letter to this cheik, and I refumed my
journey.

Having afcended a confiderable height,
I paffed a fmall wood of pines, and looked
down on the vallies of Aintoura on one
hand; and to a vaft plain bounded by the
river of Dogs, and the amphitheatrical
mountains of the Antiquefrouan, on the
other: I faw the eftate of the emir Solyma,
but the village in which he refides was covered by the interpofition of a fmall hill.

On the confines of the plain above

mentioned are the fources of the river of Dogs, which is augmented by the junction of other rivers, in their defcent from the top of the valley. Thefe fources take their rife in a very deep inner and outer cavern; the firft, formed in the rock, is of great capacity, and prefents to the eye a multitude of beautiful cryftallizations fufpended from the roof: the fecond, which is lower and more difficult of accefs, befides many other cryftals with which it is adorned, fends off one from the vault in the form of a pillar, and about the thicknefs of a man's body, to the diftance of a foot from the ground. The traveller may obferve, through a hole in the rock, the river rifing from its fource, which rufhing in a body under thofe vaft caverns, produces a tremendous noife. I proceeded to afcend a very high mountain, at the bottom of which is the refidence of a bifhop, and near its top the village of Jelton. Notwithftanding that the foil continues dry and ftony, the mulberries thrive in a furprifing manner. This village is indeed better in appearance

than

than any I have hitherto feen; though
the houfes announce any thing rather
than the manfions of cheiks, or the great
nobility of the country: their inhabitants, however, united in intereft and affection, are contented to maintain a very
frugal but independent manner of life;
their perfons fuggeft the notion of an opulent peafantry, much more than that of a
race of mighty chiefs; but from this extreme fimplicity of manners, and inexperience of luxury, refult that courage
and magnanimity by which thofe mountaineers perfevere in afferting their freedom and almoft entire independence of the
Turkifh government. They pay to the
Porte a fmall annual tribute with great
punctuality; nor have they ever been
tempted, by the natural ftrength and advantages of their fituation, to feek a
complete exemption from the Ottoman
yoke.

I alighted at the houfe of the chiek, to
whom I had a letter from the fuperior of
Aintoura; he was abroad, but I faw fome
of his family amufing themfelves under an

M 3 arbour,

arbour, who invited me with much civility to join their company; and it was not long'before I had a very hofpitable reception from the cheik himfelf: he recommended me to the care of his fon, charging him not to lofe fight of me, and to fhew me whatever was moft interefting in the country, and beft fitted to gratify my curiofity. He obliged me to pafs three days at his houfe, after which I went to vifit feveral other of this highland nobility, in whofe houfes I was regularly ferved with a collation fimilar to what had been fet before me in the female convent, and in the families of fome refugee merchants at Aintoura. I affifted at all their affemblies, which are ufually held under the fhade of trees; and was conducted in the fame eafy manner to divine fervice, and an evening party, confifting of the youth of both fexes from the neighbourhood. In this affembly, after allotting a confiderable portion of time to the amufement of converfation, one of the company reads a part of a book on fome religious fubject, and the evening
concludes

concludes with the recitation of prayers. I was furprized to find among the inhabitants of thofe mountains fo much civility, and even urbanity of manners ; the cheik's fon, in particular, who was my friend and conductor in all excurfions, difcovered a fweetnefs of temper and difpofition uncommonly interefting.

This village is fituated on a dry and ftony foil, and has the advantage of no other water than fuch as is contained in deep wells and cifterns; but its impregnable ftrength, arifing from its lofty fituation on the third gradation of this mountainous amphitheatre, was no doubt the great inducement which engaged the lords of the Quefrouan to make, choice of it for their ufual refidence.

In the cheiks is vefted the landed property of the whole country, from which they derive a certain revenue; charged, however, with a fixed fum to the emir, who, in his turn, pays a fmall annual tribute to the Porte. They adminifter juftice within the bounds of their own eftates, and affefs the people in their proportion of the

M 4 public

public burthens; but in all other refpects the diftinctions of rank are better under-ftood in Europe than among the moun-tains of the Quefrouan, where every man is at liberty to know and feel his own va-lue and confequence. The Catholics are alone regarded as the true and legitimate inhabitants of the country; and hence, on the road to Tripoli, which paffes through its lower dependencies, the Turks are fub-jected to a certain toll, from which all Chriftians are exempted.

The people are never feen at any dif-tance from their villages without being completely armed; and among them no manner of perfonal infult is ever fuffered to pafs with impunity. The countenance of a native has an expreffion of confidence in himfelf different from impudence or ef-frontery, but conveying an idea of good-nefs and affability, united to great intre-pidity of mind: he is given to compaf-fion and offices of hofpitality; gay, how-ever, and lively in his ordinary deport-ment; and he difcovers on fome occafions a confiderable talent for irony.

The clergy in this country are poor,

and labour with their own hands in fupport of their families; for though Catholics, being of a ritual different from the Latin, a man may take orders fubfequent to
his marriage, provided it had been con-
tracted with a virgin.   Here, therefore,
a prieft feldom remains long in a ftate
of celibacy, which is extremely agreeable to the tafte of his people.   Divine
fervice is celebrated in the Syriac language, but the gofpels and breviary are
read aloud in the Arabic, which is the
vulgar tongue in all countries bordering
on Arabia.   As the ftudies of the clergy
are almoft entirely confined to the fcrip-
tures and the catechifm of the church,
they are very little converfant in abftrufe
queftions of theology; but they are regular in their lives, found in their morals,
and fincere in what they believe.   Specu-
lative tenets might create a fpirit of con-
troverfy, engender new opinions, and have
a dangerous tendency to fhake their prefent implicit fubmiffion and obedience to
the fee of Rome.

Our miffionaries are extremely ufeful
here, and in other parts of Syria, not only
by

by inftructing the true Catholics, but in
converting fuch to the Latin ritual as have
been enfnared in the erroneous opinions of
fchifm or herefy. The Catholic faith has
made confiderable progrefs at Damafcus,
as well as in the parts S. W. from the
mountains, where the Syrians, Greeks,
and Arminians, ufed to be few, compared with fchifmatics and heretics of different denominations. The religion of
Rome has alfo, by the fame means, penetrated into Egypt, where I am informed a number of Cophti have fub-
mitted to the doctrines and authority of
the church. Some of them, however,
in deference to the manners and cuftoms
of their country, admit of circumcifion in
both fexes, a practice in direct oppofition to a decree exprefsly paffed againft it
in the court of Rome.

It is to be hoped that the pious induftry of thefe men may ftill extend
the fphere of its operation, particularly on the fide of Abyffinia, where, confidering the frequency, fimplicity, and
honefty of Chriftian heretics, there is
every

every reafon to believe that the truly apof-
tolic miffionary might reap a confiderable
harveft.   I have had occafion to obferve
the unwearied pains taken by this defcrip-
tion of men, in Turky, Perfia, and the nations of India, all abounding in Chriftians ill
inftructed, and without the means of better information—how fincerely it is to be
regretted that their number is fo very
fmall! Confidering the many difcourage-
ments the miffionary meets with in the
Eaft, from regulations of national police, one
cannot fufficiently admire his fuccefs in the
kingdoms of Pegu, Siam, Cambodia, Cochin-
china, and China.   A few natives of China,
who were educated fome time fince in an Italian feminary, have rendered eminent fervices
to their countrymen in matters of religion.

The anfwer made by the king of Spain,
to one who urged the impolicy of re-
taining poffeffion of the Philippine ifles,
from the heavy expence they incurred to
the public, deferves to be recorded: He
defired, he faid, no other produce from
thefe iflands than the fruits of his miffion;
and he would be fatisfied if, among the

4   millions

millions of Chriftian profelytes, added to the
church fince their firft fubmiffion to the
crown of Spain, there were one poor Indian,
whófe name fhould be found at laft written in
the book of life. It may be juftly faid of
Spain, that fhe has made more Chriftians
in Afia and America than fhe has fubjects
in the whole extent of her European dominions.—But I return to the Quefrouan.

The impregnable fituation of this country having naturally pointed it out as an
afylum for all the profeffors of Chriftianity in Afiatic Turky, it has become the
refidence of many bifhops, and the feat of
a confiderable number of convents for both
fexes. Among the former are the patriarch
of the Greek church; the patriarch of Antioch, who prefides over the Maronitic
fect; and the patriarch of Armenia, who
fuperintends feveral convents under the
rules of his own ritual. The people in
general are fond of religion; and though
vice and immorality find their way into
all countries, they are, however, much
lefs prevalent in the mountains than in
the plain. The fex do not live under

3

der the fame rigorous difcipline, nor are
they fecluded from public view nearly
in the fame degree as in the towns; but
if an unmarried woman has the misfortune
to become pregnant, fhe expiates with her
life, and by the hands of her own relations, the folly and weaknefs of her conduct. A mother who has given her
daughter in marriage, would confider herfelf and family greatly difhonoured, if after
confummation her fon-in-law fhould not
produce proofs of the virtue of his bride.
A like cuftom prevails among the natives
of Mexico.

I left Jelton on the third day after my
arrival; and, conceiving that the moft
elevated ridges, being little frequented by
ftrangers, muft prefent the manners of the
people in their true and genuine colours,
I took the route towards Mafra, a village
fituated at the foot of the higheft mountain in the Quefrouan, and where the natives feed their flocks in the fummer feafon. After an hour's walk I afcended to a
convent amidft difmal and arid rocks,
whence,

whence, however, iffues a plentiful fpring
of water, which diffufes moifture and a
charming verdure over all the foil in their
vicinity. The vivid green of thefe earthy
patches, and the brown parched furface of
the rocks, which briftle like needles in the
air all around, form a ftriking contraft to
the eye. In the monaftery, however, fituated in the centre of this horrid fcene,
a right reverend prelate has chofen to take
up his abode.

I afcended confiderably higher, and, arriving at the village of *Claat*, where the
foil is fertile, lefs ftony, and covered with
trees in a frefh and thriving ftate, I refted
fome time, in company with a cheik of
humane and obliging manners. Having
refumed my journey, after walking half an
hour I came to the confines of a valley,
where I looked down a precipice to a narrow glen, fcarce affording room for a large
torrent, which rolled its waters with great
noife and impetuofity over immenfe fragments of rocks. I defcended on foot,
and having croffed the torrent at a bridge
clofe to a water-mill, I began to climb a
mountain

mountain on the oppofite fide, which I found particularly difficult. I was a good deal fatigued before I reached the top; but at laft perfeverance brought me to the profpect of a beautiful country, planted with the fineft mulberries I had yet feen. Springs in abundance diftil from the heights upon a fertile foil, without a ftone, and prefenting over the wide extent of this natural amphitheatre a neat and even furface. Under the mulberries, the ground produces roots and vegetables of different kinds. I at laft arrived at the village of Mafra, fituated on the declivity of a high hill, which appears every where ftudded with houfes, and at the diftance of three leagues and a half from Jelton. I was much pleafed with the beauty of the fcene, and little repined at the toil I had experienced in climbing up to my prefent elevated fituation.

The cheik at Jelton having given me a letter to the minifter of the parifh, I alighted at his door. He was not at home, but I was admitted to his wife and feveral of his children. The good woman received

received me in the beſt manner, preſſed
me to wait her huſband's return, and to
repoſe myſelf after my fatigue.   I began
to obſerve, with the moſt pleaſant emotions,
the wife of the ſimple paſtor of Mafra,
who was at this moment working in his
field, and who I had no doubt was ſoon
to enter his porch in an equally ruſtic
appearance with that of his ſpouſe.   She
was a fine woman, in the flower of
her youth, conſiderably advanced in her
pregnancy, and with a complexion deep-
ly browned in the ſun.   In the midſt
of three little children, whom ſhe endeavoured to quiet by turns, ſhe conducted the detail of her little family affairs.   How much I admired this pre-
cious and ſimple manner of living!   In
a kind of open gallery, which ſerved
for a parlour, ſhe ſpread a little bed on
the ground, in order to lay her infant
to ſleep; caſting her eye occaſionally to a
ſtove, where ſhe boiled ſome ſlices of
gourd in a kettle.   She dreſſed ſome eggs
and milk in ſeparate diſhes, with crape-
cakes, for my ſupper.   At one time ſhe
feemed

feemed to affure me by her looks of all
the inclination in the world to entertain
me well; at another fhe could not conceal her impatience for her hufband. Meanwhile the good man arrived from his farm;
and his attentions to his gueft feemed
to vie with the kind civilities he had
juft received from his wife. In compliance, however, with the reftraints
Oriental manners impofe on the behaviour of women, fhe foon withdrew, and
gave up her whole attention to the concerns of her little family. At the hour
for evening *vefpers*, the people affembled
in the open air, where prayers were recited as much in the fpirit of true piety,
and confequently in a manner equally ac-
ceptable in the eye of the Deity, as if we
had been feated under the gilded ceiling
of the moft fumptuous temple. His flock
feemed defirous of my company, and were
at pains to difcover by what means they
might amufe me moft agreeably.

The fall of night brought home a number
of domeftic animals in flocks, which confti-
tuted the whole wealth of this honeft eccle-

fiaftic

fiaftic. His wife and him fed them by hand,
and received their careffes, the only return
their inferior natures could make for the care
and kindnefs of their mafters ; a fituation,
however, extremely interefting, and which
tends to illuftrate thofe gentle and innocent
difpofitions fo prevalent among the Afiatics.

At my own defire, my bed was laid in
a raifed corner under the porch, and my hoft
repofed clofe by me and my conductor;
for, according to the manners of the mountaineers, the mafter of a family is himfelf
the keeper and guardian of his guefts ; a
rule of hofpitality which was religioufly obferved refpecting me by the cheik's fon at
Jelton.   Befides, as the cuftoms of the
Eaft do not permit ftrangers to fleep under
the fame roof with the women, vifitors
are always lodged under the porch, or in the
apartments named Manfoul, which have
no communication whatever with the principal part of the houfe.   I refted extremely well ; but, owing to the cold and keen
air of thefe lofty mountains, which are a
continuation

continuation of the famous Mount Lebanon, I caught a flight rheumatifm, which,
however, the genial warmth of the next
day entirely removed.

As foon as it was day, I attended my
hoft to the celebration of mafs; after
which, notwithftanding the moft prefling
invitation to prolong my vifit, I refumed
my journey, and proceeded towards what
is efteemed the higheft mountain in the
country.   On account of the winter fnows
there is no human habitation higher than
the village of Mafra, which is itfelf covered with fnow during fix months of the
year.

We pafled the fkirts of fome mulberry plantations belonging to Mafra, where
the foil continues of equal fertility, and
well watered, with few ftones.   Upon
afcending, however, a mountain of moderate height, the mulberry entirely difap-
pears, a circumftance probably owing to
the foil's being feverely chilled by the
continuance of the fnow.   I now came to
land in a ftate of nature, grazed by cattle
of various kinds, which, a little farther on,

N 2   the

the natives are ufed to fold during the night. I obferved fheep-folds, for the firft time, on the top of a little hill, whofe fides were fown with different kinds of grain. The fhepherds are employed in making cheefe of the milk they obtain in the morning; and here I ftopped to breakfaft, in company with feveral inhabitants of Mafra.

I was now conducted a little higher to a rich and fertile plain, a fhort league in length, and only a quarter in breadth, which was fown in the fame manner as the hill I have mentioned, and prefented a moft pleafing verdure to the eye. This extenfive field is bounded towards the fouth by the great mountain, whofe perpendicular rocks are loft in the clouds; towards the eaft and north by a fmall hill; while towards the weft the eye flits over fucceffive chains of mountains to a great diftance. I furveyed the ruins of an ancient tower, in form nearly a fquare, and built of huge ftones, fome of which, having their extremities fixed in oppofite walls, were of length fufficient

to

to anſwer the purpoſe of beams, while others were employed as lintils to the gates inſtead of arches. Over the firſt gate is an inſcription in Greek charaƈters, which it was not in my power to tranſcribe; but, in an angle of the building, on the outſide, I found another, of which I obtained a perfeƈt copy, and which the Academy of Sciences at Paris have taken the trouble to tranſlate: it marks the period in which the tower was ereƈted, and not the age of the temple I am ſoon to ſpeak of, which is probably much more ancient, but concerning which it likewiſe makes mention.

ΓΕ ΝΤΕΠΙΤΘΑΜ ΡΑΒ ΒΟΜΟΥ ΕΠΜΕΑΗ-
ΤΟΥ ΕΚΤωΝΤΟΥ ΜΕΠΣΤΟΥ ΘΕΟΥ
ωΚΟΔΟ ΜΗΘΗ.
(doubtful)

" In the three hundred and fifty-fifth " year, Tholmus preſiding for the ſixth " time over the Temple of the Moſt High " God, this Building was ereƈted." The period alluded to by this inſcription is the æra of the Seleucides, that is, three hun-

dred

dred and twelve years before the birth of
Jefus Chrift. Thefe ruins extend from the
tower weftward on the ample field already
defcribed, and conduct the traveller to others
of greater magnitude. The firft object
here that fixed my attention was a ftone,
which in its fize and fhape feemed to have
been employed as the bafe of an altar.
Befide it lay another, in the centre of whofe
plane appeared a raifed quadrangular fpace,
furrounded by a groove; this ftone, with
equal probability, might have ferved as
the table of the altar. I next obferved
the remains of a very wide gate, which
externally had two galleries fronting each
other. At the end of either gallery is a
large open hall, adorned with pillars, whofe
capitals, ornamented with flowers and
foliage in excellent fculpture, are ftrong
indications of the great extent and magnificence of this very ancient building.
Within the gate, and in the middle of a
large area, my conductor fhewed me a
well of extraordinary depth. At the oppofite end of the temple is a gallery,
which occupies the whole breadth of the
building,

building, and is fupported by a row of mafly pillars, fimilar to thofe already mentioned. Beyond this gallery are the ruins of a wall, and an area of a very large room, at the bottom of which lay other ruins, but I was unable to difco-ver what was under them, or whether they did not feparate us from another hall.

This very ancient and venerable temple is now almoft in ruins; the pillars, and a great proportion of the walls, lie fcattered in large fragments on the ground. Its fcite is amidft high perpendicular rocks, which in fome places ferved it for ramparts. Ac-cording to the natives it was a temple, confecrated to the mother of the gods, un-der the reign of one of the Ptolemies, but which they cannot pretend to fay; a tra-dition, however, which has probably been perverted in the circumftance wherein it differs from the interpretation given of the infcription by the learned academy, efpe-cially as the only variety between them con-fifts in the word *mother* inftead of *father*, and thefe in the Arabic may be very eafily

N 4   confounded.

confounded. The diftrict in which thefe ruins are to be found is called, in the dialect of the country, Elfogra. It was in this quarter of Lebanon, if we may give credit to the tradition of the natives, where thofe ftately cedars grew, which were conveyed to Jerufalem, and ufed in the conftruction of Solomon's temple. However this may be, this auguft edifice, having the fame advantages of view with the adjacent plain, was erected in a moft delightful fituation.

From the ruins I accompanied my conductor to a rich fpring of fine limpid water, on the brink of which we fat down to dinner. Such is the very cold temperature of this water, that I was unable to hold my hand in it for any length of time. Several of the villagers of Mafra having favoured me with their company on this expedition, our provifions were a joint ftock, and after making an agreeable repaft we continued our progrefs to the right of the great mountain. The rocks contained Greek infcriptions; but as thefe confifted only of

two

two or three letters, I did not take the trouble to tranfcribe them.

Afcending eaftward, in the fame direction, we came to other ruins, fome of whofe ftones feemed perforated for the infertion of pipes, which might in former times have ferved for a fountain or jet-d'eau. Thefe, therefore, were probably the ruins of an object, which had been erected as a *vifta* to the temple, in the bottom of the plain.

Having reached the top of the hill, we found ourfelves on the Afs's Back, which flopes on one fide into the plain, and on the other into a vale of great depth. Along this ridge runs a canal, which ferves to conduct the water to Mafra, which I faw there in fuch plenty. I traced it for a quarter of a league, and came to a very fteep mountain, where we found the copious fource, whofe bottom we could not perceive: from this refervoir two canals, each of which might contain three cubic feet, receive their ample fupplies; but fuch is the intenfe cold of this water, that in drinking it one is in

danger

danger of lofing his teeth; and I was apprehenfive it might affect my bowels. I have been fince told, what feems extremely probable, that thefe fprings are fed by the fnows of more northern mountains, which are melted by the fun, and afterwards filtrated through the rocks.

At the diftance of about two leagues from Mafra, the higher grounds being wholly uninhabited, I parted with my companions, who chofe to return to the village, and took a little refrefhment and repofe. They went back to Mafra; but though I meant to return to the fame place, I chofe to follow a different route, by the other branch of the canal, which fets off from the above-mentioned fource.

My way foon led me to a natural arch, about forty paces broad, and four-fcore in length, than which I never faw a more majeftic fpecimen of nature's workmanfhip, or more nearly approaching in many refpects to the execution of art. The waters pouring from the heights during the

melting

melting of the fnow, gradually unite in
a great torrent, which precipitating itfelf
forms a cafcade about forty feet high, pur-
fues its courfe with increafed rapidity
amongft rifted rocks, and at length paffes
under this arch, fifty paces perhaps below
the fall.   The vault of the arch, though
on a level with the road, is at leaft one
hundred feet above the bed of the torrent, which here begins to enter the mouth
of a little valley. The oppofite banks ferve
as abutments to the extremities of the
arch, which has all the neatnefs of effect
expected from the fkill and dexterity of an
architect. It is difficult to fay by what
means nature, after having penetrated the folid mafs of fteep rocks, contrived to fmooth
and polifh this into the form of a fine arch,
with all the regularity and precifion of the
chizzel : probably the violence of the current firft made an impreffion on the lefs
compact parts at its bafe, where having at
length pierced and undermined the huge
block, it afterwards gradually filed it away
in this uniform manner, from an equal de-

7   gree

gree of refiftance being every where op-
pofed to the force of the torrent.

Paffing this curious arch, and making a fweep round the fide of the mountain, I entered fome pleafant and fertile
fields. In a recefs of the mountain I faw
the fources of the river *la Croix*, which I
had paffed in my way to Mafra. Keeping
ftill on the fkirts of the mountain, I
paffed in view of various beautiful caf-
cades, and came to a large valley well
watered, and producing a kind of fmall
grain. La Croix, befides fupplying a canal cut along the declivity of the oppofite
mountain, furnifhes water to two others
of a larger fize. Croffing this valley I afcended a high earthy hill, where the
foil becomes more fandy, and lefs fertile,
than in the preceding parts of my excurfion. Turning off to the right, I arrived at a handfome village, whence we
have a view of Mafra, fituated on a neighbouring eminence. This hamlet is in the
vicinity of a place named *Haragges,* and
furrounded with fine mulberries excellently fupplied with moifture. I paffed fome

poor

poor ftony ground, little fufceptible of cultivation; and left on my right a number
of fmall vallies, apparently of great fertility. I now arrived on the borders of a little
plain, on which ftand a church and convent
containing only one monk and a friar, detached in the manner of a little colony
from a more populous monaftery : here we
paffed the night, and had no reafon to
complain of our entertainment. Next day
after mafs, having breakfafted, for in this
country it is againft every rule of hofpitality to fuffer a ftranger to depart without eating, we refumed our journey, and
paffed over a miferable foil, covered fometimes with a dead fand, and fometimes
with| arge ftones, fimilar to what we had
feen the preceding evening. The produce of this diftrict was chiefly pines,
and herds of goats. At nine o'clock we
faw a handfome church, at a village called Befommar, which is the refidence of
the Armenian patriarch. After paying
refpects to his eminence, I took fome refrefhment, and continued my journey. I
defcended lower on the mountain, and
then

then turned to the right, entering upon a ſtrong ſoil, in all reſpects like that of Aintoura and Jelton. Deſcending to a ſecond ridge, which commands a proſpect of the ſea, I ſaw the village of Agouſta below, and on our right at ſome diſtance that of Gazir. In the firſt, beſides ſeveral cheiks, reſides the venerable patriarch of the Maronitic ſect of Antioch, at whoſe manſion I ſtopped, and was received with much politeneſs and affection. I had the honour to dine with this good man, who in the courſe of our converſation ſpoke Latin and Italian with great correctneſs and fluency. One of his grand vicars favoured me with conſtant attendance, and about four o'clock, when the patriarch awaked from his nap, I took an affectionate leave. We walked round the village, which is moſt agreeably ſituated on the declivity of a very high mountain, cultivated in the form of a wild amphitheatre, and interſperſed with gardens and mulberry plantations. The houſes are ſcattered all over the area of a horſe-ſhoe, with its opening towards the ſea, for ſuch is the

appearance

appearance of the mountain, and extend
down to the bottom, where the ground
rifes into another ridge, which is well watered, and ftill very high above the plain.
The whole of this mountain is well cultivated; and in the middle of the village,
oppofite to the houfe of a cheik, is a copious fpring of excellent water. The fituation of this village is extremely beautiful;
but fometimes about noon clouds, attract-
ed by the lofty tops of the mountains, produce an obfcurity, and a thick mift, which
I apprehend is infalubrious.

Quitting the village, I croffed the mountain, paffed a ftony barren region, and
came in view of the hofpice of Ariffa,
which belongs to the fathers of the Holy
Land, or the Recollects of St. Francis. After an hour's walk from Agoufta, I arrived at this religious manfion.   The
hofpice or convent is fituated on the fummit of a mountain, at a little diftance
from the fea, of which it commands an
extenfive profpect; but ftanding upon a
poor foil, and having no water, except
what is preferved in cifterns, it is upon the
whole

whole a barren and dreary retreat. I departed next day early, and after defcending towards the inland country, and travelling in the fkirts of the mountains,
which are extremely painful and difficult,
I at laft reached a narrow dale watered by
a beautiful rivulet. I afcended on the other
fide, and fkirted the mountains, and foon
came in fight of Aintoura, prefenting itfelf on an adjacent hill. The intervening
ground is very uneven, but not fo wild
and rugged as the high mountain I had
juft traverfed. I arrived at Aintoura on
the fixth day; and having, after dinner,
thanked the fuperior for all his kind offices, I began to defcend towards the
plain.

I reached Baruth in the evening, after
an abfence of ten days, which had been
fpent in exploring the mountains of the
Quefrouan. The prior of the Capuchin
convent received me with his ufual civility; from him I learned that a king's
chebec had arrived from France on a
cruize off the coaft of Syria. Having obtained further information that this veffel,
then

then at the island of Cyprus, was expected
in a few days to enter the port of Sidon;
and as that city was only distant eight
leagues, I proposed instantly to set out,
in hopes of meeting some old companions, with whom I had served at
Toulon. Accordingly, on the 25th of
August, I proceeded to Sidon, and waited
upon the French consul, who shewed me
much kindness, and offered to accommo-
date me with quarters in his house. He
confirmed the prior's information respecting
the arrival of a French chebeck; but I
got notice some days after, that she had
quitted Cyprus, and was sailed for Candia,
in order to join other ships of the same
division. Disappointed in my views, I resolved to proceed directly to Acre, per-
suaded that the frequent arrivals there
from the port of Marseilles must render my passage to France much less precarious.

My fame as a traveller seemed to have
made some impression on the mind of
the consul, for he made many enquiries
concerning my late expedition, and pref-

fed me to fpend a little time longer in his family; urging, as reafons for my compliance, the extreme fatigue I had fuffered in the defert, and the deranged ftate of my conftitution. He obferved that the remains of an eruption on my fkin, which had made its appearance in the country of the Marrattas, proved that my blood was greatly heated; and as I was defirous to ftudy the character of their mountaineers, I ought to confider them more extenfively, and avoid forming a hafty opinion from a curfory view, or rather from the appearance of a few individuals. Although a long feclufion from the company of women had produced in me a rufticity of manners as well as appearance, his wife feemed to be of the fame mind with her hufband, and united in entreaties that I would remain their gueft for fome time longer. The refolution I had taken, to fail directly for France, began to be fhaken. The weak ftate of my health, an eruption on my fkin, and above all, the additional pleafure I had in profpect among thefe mountains, feemed on this occafion to fufpend the

the ordinary vigour of my mind; and frefh knowledge, fo agreeable to my tafte, which I hoped to acquire in my intercourfe with the neighbouring Arabs, apologized for what, however, I could not help tacitly regarding as a facility of temper. About a month after my arrival I was feized with a regular fever; but the ufe of emetics, and the great care and attention of the conful and his family, gradually reftored me to health.

In the environs of Sidon the eye is delighted with the delicious verdure of many fine profpects; the rich gardens and orchards, which are excellently watered, diffufe over the face of the country the appearance of one continued foreft, confifting of various fruit-trees, together with the vine, which is permitted to grow here in all its luxuriance:

In the mountains of the neighbourhood are many caverns excavated in the rocks, with ten or twelve cells in each, according to their fize. Thefe, according to tradition, are the tombs of the ancient inhabitants of Sidon; but I am rather inclined to believe

they

they were places of retreat for the natives of the mountains. A caftle is fhewn built by St. Louis;—fome pillars of marble and floors of jafper in Mofaic, are the principal remains of antiquity that now exift of this once beautiful and flourifhing city.

On the ifland of Java are feveral mofques, fcarce meriting the attention of the curious; but in the vicinity of this town I obtained accefs to a very confiderable one. The building is of a quadrangular form, and is erected, like all other mofques, according to the direction of its place relatively to Mecca. The firft object I remarked is a rail at the bottom of the mofque, within which is contained a model of Abraham's houfe at Mahomet's grave. Rows of lamps, ornamented with oftrich's eggs, appear fufpended from the ceiling, at the diftance of feven or eight feet from the ground. The floor is covered with a clean handfome mat for the proftrations of believers; a religious ceremony which they conftantly perform with the face towards Mecca. This mode of doration confifts in quick and frequent proftrations,

proftrations, and does not in all probability owe its origin to Mahomet, fince in the Chriftian worfhip of thofe parts we find it practifed nearly in the fame manner: it is however, an expreffion of piety and devotion, of a nature noble and majeftic, and highly fuitable to thofe fentiments it is meant to exprefs.

Befides ftudying the rules and principles of the Arabic language, in which I was foon able to difcover much beauty, I was at pains to obtain every information in my power relative to the manners of the people who live among the adjacent mountains. That diftrict which lies towards the S. W. is inhabited by a fect of Muffulmen, who are named *Mutuallis*, and are faid to have no connection with any other nation whatever. They obferve the fame diftance and referve towards ftrangers as the natives of India, neither inviting them to their houfes, nor eating with them from the fame difh; and though I cannot complain of having received the flighteft injury during the time I paffed in their villages, I own, in their appearance, they

.O 3   have

have fomething peculiarly rude and ferocious. They tolerate Chriftians in the free
exercife of their religion, who, happily,
are much lefs the objects of their hatred
and animofity than the Turks. Their
dominion extends over the mountains all
the way from Gebail to Balbec, including
both towns, where they are reported to be
much more favage in their manners than in
the vicinity of Sidon. The mountains in the
N. E. of Sidon are peopled by the Drufes,
among whom Chriftianity enjoys an equal
degree of toleration as among the Mutuallis.

The natives in thefe mountains are difaffected to the Turks, an antipathy partly
owing to the influence of inveterate prejudice, and partly to a difference in matters of
religious opinion. They are fenfible it is
to their own bravery, and the inacceffible
nature of their mountains, that they owe
their happy independence. The Drufes
are well affected towards Chriftians in
general; but holding themfelves defcended from a French anceftry, who are faid
to have taken refuge in thefe mountains

†   at

at their expulſion from the Holy Land, in the end of the cruſades, they have more than ordinary affection for the people of that country. The principles which, according to hiſtorians, actuated the ſubjects of the old man of the mountain, ſtill influence the minds of ſome individuals.

In the vicinity of Jeruſalem I am told there is a race of Bedouin Arabs, who likewiſe affect to be deſcended from the French. The Capuchin from whom I had this information had experienced many inſtances of their partiality to his country, as well as a miſſionary of the ſame order, who reſided among them for ſome time in much credit and eſteem.

I was charmed with the beauty and ſerenity of this climate, which, in my opinion, is in a peculiar manner what a man who is deſirous of becoming the child of nature would wiſh to enjoy. In the different regions of the globe which I have viſited I have found no climate equally propitious to the natural ſtate of man with that which extends its mild influence over the

O 4   ſouthern

fouthern parts of Syria. In the countries fituated between the tropics the rains fall almoft inceffantly during fix months of fummer; the countries, on the contrary, a few
degrees without the tropics, have but little
rain, and that only in fpring and autumn, the
feafons when it paffes from cold to hotter
regions of the earth. In Afia, on the confines of Baffora; in America, in the vicinity of Sartille; as well as in the defert
regions of Africa, I have had occafion to
remark that fcarcity of rain, rendering the
foil dry and inhofpitable, gradually re-
duces it to a dead fand. I will not pretend to fay, however, that from this par-
tial obfervation any rule can be drawn
that fhall obtain univerfally; but the fact
feems to be, that from the latitude of
thirty to thirty-five degrees, the fummer
fix months are entirely exempted from
rain; whilft in the fucceeding period the
cold is uniformly moderate, and one meets
with many intervals of fine weather equal
to the moft beautiful days in fummer.

In Syria a variety of grain fprings and
comes

comes to maturity during the winter months;
a fact which affords undeniable evidence
of what I have now been afferting. I ac-
knowledge there are certain fpecies of
trees which then fhed their leaves; ftill,
however, it is true, that in the month of
November I have eaten new beans and
peafe, while the gardens, abounding in
flowers and vegetables, continue to produce
from that month till the opening of fummer. The particular fituation of Syria
contributes a great deal to the excellency
of the climate : it is protected from the
north wind by an extenfive ridge of lofty
mountains; it is bounded on the weft by
the fea; and on the eaft with the arid deferts of Arabia, from whofe parched and
fandy foil little vapour can arife to produce rain. The higher Egypt, as well as
the country contiguous to Lima, are fine-
ly fituated; but I believe the one and the
other owe their dry and beautiful climates
to fome high ridges, which intercept the
progrefs of the clouds. In the neighbourhood of Lima the foil is fandy and barren,
while Egypt owes her fertility to the induftry

duſtry of her inhabitants, joined to the annual inundations of the Nile. Beſides,
the heat of ſummer in the higher Egypt
is almoſt intolerable; and every one knows
that the Cophti as well as the Peruvian,
groaning under the oppreſſion of deſpotiſm,
are highly taxed for their advantages of
climate.

Among the productions of Syria are
thoſe of hot as well as cold climates;
wheat, barley, cotton, the bamy or gom-
beau, the oak, the pine, and the ſycamore,
all grow in a great degree of perfection.
The vine, the fig, the mulberry, the apple,
and other trees of Europe, are no leſs common in the gardens and orchards, than
the jujubier, the fig-bannan, the lemon,
ſweet and four, the orange, and the ſugar-
cane: all the roots and vegetable productions of theſe different climates are likewiſe found here in abundance.

The rites and ceremonies of the Catholic church are as regularly and openly exer-
ciſed in the boſom of the Syrian mountains, as in Paris or at Rome; with this difference, however, that as the manners of
the

the people are more fimple, fo their devotion, as well as their morals, are proportionally purer in the former than in the
latter.

The induftrious character of the natives
appears in the cultivated ftate of their
mountains, many parts of which prefent
the face of a fine garden. Springs, ju-
dicioufly directed, water their mulberry
plantations, in which confift the wealth
of the country; and fuch is the fuperior
quality and high value of the filk raifed
from the mulberry-leaves, that the farmer
obtains by his trees, at little expence or
labour, a competent fubfiftence for his family : wine, oil, and figs, are articles from
which he likewife derives confiderable
emolument.

We do not meet here with any thing
to compare with the riches and luxury
of European nations; but as the for-
tunes of individuals are lefs unequal, po-
verty and indigence, which confume the
loweft clafs of the people in the fineft
provinces of France, are altogether unknown.

If

If any perfon wifhed to know where man is fubjected to the leaft penury and wretchednefs, I would refer him to the mountains of Syria, where the refinements in luxury are indeed precluded, but where he would amply enjoy every thing necef-fary to his peace and happinefs. The powers of the mind are not chilled and exafperated by the feverities of an inhof-pitable climate, neither are they debaf-ed and enervated by the fecure poffeffion of unfolicited abundance. Subfiftence, though eafy, is not, however, to be ob-tained without bodily fatigue, which tends only to brace and ftrengthen the limbs. The avocations of the people are entertaining to the mind, at the fame time that they are beneficial to the body, and divert them from any defire for gratifications which are only neceffary to the happinefs of thofe devoted to ha-bits of idlenefs and intemperance. Who-ever looks forward to a ftate of vacan-cy and idlenefs as the period when he fhall begin to enjoy life, would, were he

ever

ever to attain it, probably find himfelf
miferably difappointed. Moderate labour,
and a temperate diet, rendering the body healthy and robuft, impart alfo vigour
to the mind; and hence arifes that fine
relifh for thofe innocent pleafures which
delight the induftrious man after fatigue, more than is ever experienced by
his wealthier but more indolent neighbour.

Nocte fatigatum fomnus, non cura puellæ,
Excepit; et pingui membra quiete levat.

In vain would the traveller expect to
meet, in thofe mountains, with men of
great learning, or of very polifhed and
refined manners; but he will find men
in their beft and happieft ftate, men
purfuing their duty from the impulfe
of natural fentiment, firm friends, good
fathers, virtuous citizens; and fuch characters are of more benefit to the world
than the rich, idle, and luxurious, who in
more refined countries contaminate the
manners of the people by their example,
without

without contributing in any degree to the real interests of mankind,

The monks of Syria are neither profound theologians, nor extremely rigid in their manners; the rules of their orders are simple, and scrupulously observed; but they are in reality what they affect to be in appearance, humble servants and disciples of their Master, and earn their daily bread by honest labour, and the industry of their hands.

The secular clergy have little either of learning or rank to be distinguished from the vulgar; but though their knowledge is chiefly confined to the New Testament, they are men of regular and pious lives, and highly esteemed by their flocks. Little indebted to the emoluments of a liberal public establishment, they earn by toil, and the sweat of their brows, a subsistence for their wives and children. They give constant attendance to the service of the altar, preach the gospel to the poor, and enforce the Christian morality by their example, to which the
abolition

abolition of celibacy among them has been of advantage. The attention they beſtow on the education of their own families furniſhes an important leſſon to thoſe who are leſs immediately under their eye. I have always conſidered marriage as a natural duty, and conſtituting one of the inalienable rights of mankind.

The laws and maxims of policy that obtain in ſuch countries as were firſt peopled appear to me, in general, to be the beſt ; but no laws or inſtitutions, how wiſely ſoever ſuggeſted, are able to reſtrain the deſires of men aſſembled in great cities : in the country alone the traveller may hope to diſcover their original meaning and intention. There the peaſant, removed from the depraved ſociety of the citizen, from the improper diſpoſal of his time, and every means of corruption, implicitly follows the laws and cuſtoms of his anceſtors.

It is a maxim with eaſtern nations, that a man ſhall be bound by the obligations of marriage, without any previous acquaintance with his intended wife. Now, few inſtitutions inftitutions can immediately appear more whimfical and abfurd; in experience, however, the inconveniences we might think incident to fuch a practice are not felt; and I am fatisfied, from all I have ob-ferved in the families of the mountaineers, amongft whom I made it my bufinefs to refide, that the feuds and animofi-ties of domeftic life are much lefs fre-quent there than in the countries of Eu-rope. It is likewife ufual in India to marry at the age of eight or ten, and a girl is generally betrothed to a particular hufband at the age of three or four; and I repeat, that in my experience I had the good fortune never to meet with a fingle couple who feemed to have been injudi-cioufly or unhappily paired. Educated to-gether from the years of childhood, they become familiar with each other's humours, acquire the character of fituation, and are not likely to experience in advanced life any thing that can reafonably give occafion to furprize. The hufband exercifes domi-nion over his companion, while fhe ufes with fuccefs, in her turn, her natural weapons

of

of tears, gentlenefs, and fubmiffion. Thus, between a couple of Afiatics, born, as it would feem, with a kind of innate rectitude of mind, we naturally expect the moft happy and cordial union. Refpecting the liberty of free choice, in which the ftrength of the argument on our fide feems to confift, I am afraid that in the tender and inexperienced mind there frequently fprings from this very fource a love of variety; for the woman who conceives herfelf entitled to chufe in one inftance, may fee little harm in exercifing the fame right a fecond time, provided fhe happens to meet with another perfon whofe character is better fitted to engage her affections.

It is an opinion pretty generally received in the nations of Afia, that the morals of the women have much influence on fociety at large, as well as on their own children. But they have an idea, perhaps a little more peculiar to themfelves, to wit, that the quality and intenfity of fentiment in our fex refult partly from the allurements of pleafure, partly from prejudice and habit, and partly from the dread of thofe evils

VOL. II.   P   which

which tend to the deftruction of the individual. Defire, hope, love, hatred, and, in general, all our fentiments and actions, depend, according to them, upon a felfifh principle of fear, which, in proportion as we are impreffed with the danger of defeat, or the hope of victory, produces weaknefs or courage.

But of fuch as confider fear or an interefted concern for our own welfare, as the ultimate principle of human fentiment and conduct, I would afk, Whether a mother's fondnefs for her child, as the Afiatics feem to believe, contains no ingredient of a more liberal origin than that fweet fenfation of pleafure fhe experiences at the end of her labour, when fhe reflects that her fufferings were occafioned by a being which makes a part of herfelf, and therefore entitled to her kindeft affections? Muft the gradual increafe of paternal affection be referred folely to habit, and the attachment one neceffarily acquires for an object which cofts him much care and anxiety? In the fame manner is the fentiment of friendfhip, a fentiment equally

equally rare and valuable, to be refolved
into habit, or the hope of deriving advantage from our friend? Are pity, charity,
and beneficence, which are excited by
the misfortunes of others, of no higher account than that of a mean reflex fentiment
on our own condition? In a word, are magnanimity, generofity, and courage, nothing
better than different modifications of the
fame interefted principle, congratulating
itfelf on having efcaped thofe evils which
we wifh to alleviate in others?—This fyf-
tem is too humiliating to the human fpecies
to be founded in the conftitution of nature.

In Arabia, and in all countries with
which the Arabs have intercourfe, the
women are fubjected to the veil, and almoft entirely fecluded from the company
of the men. Each fex lives apart, and in
conformity to its own humours; infomuch that the hufband fpends but a fmall
part of his time with his wife. This cuftom is confidered as extremely beneficial to
both parties; for, as the object of marriage
is mutual fidelity, the great danger incident to happinefs in that ftate is to be

apprehend-

apprehended from eafy and frequent communication between the fexes : and as the
temper and difpofitions of a man and his
wife do not at all times coalefce, the fel-
domer they meet the fewer occafions will
occur of domeftic ftrife and animofity.
Hence they conclude that nothing can be
expected from unreftrained intercourfe be-
twixt the fexes, but exceffes of paffion in
the one, danger to the innocence of the
other, and multiplied caufes of contention
in both. Accordingly, the only perfons of
different fexes who enjoy any fhare of focial
intercourfe, are fuch as ftand in the neareft
degrees of confanguinity; a pleafure, however, which is permitted even to them fpar-
ingly and on rare occafions. In many families thefe maxims of referve are fo ftrictly
obferved, that as foon as boys attain the years
of thirteen or fourteen, they are removed to
a particular wing of the building, named
Manfoul, which is entirely unconnected with
the female apartments.

Men in eaftern nations are extremely
jealous of their fuperiority over the female fex; and hence it is that a man
feldom condefcends to eat with his wife.

It

It is her bufinefs to ferve her hufband at table with all the care and affiduity of a fervant ; nor does fhe find herfelf at liberty to fit down to a meal until he is done. He never defires her opinion, or deigns to converfe with her on the fubject of family affairs. He feldom affigns her a tafk that may not be performed without ftirring abroad, nor any bufinefs abroad but what may be performed under her veil. Women in every condition of life are fubjected to thefe regulations, and their time is all equally employed with their children and houfehold affairs, which, however, from their plain and fimple manners, require little application. I almoft revolted againft this flavifh and fubordinate condition of the fex. But I was ftruck with the great fimilarity I difcovered in this point between the manners of the American favages and thofe of the Arabs, as well as other Afiatic tribes ; a refemblance extremely furprifing, when we confider the great diftance the Arab and American are removed from each other. In America the favage charges himfelf with nothing but his

P 3

gun,

gun, while his wife follows behind him
loaded with every article of the family baggage. In Afia it is the fame : the favage en-
tertains no converfation whatever with his
wife ; nor does fhe prefume to be prefent at
any of his parties. The fame are the manners of Syria, and indeed of the Afiatic
continent in general. In the Biffayan ifles,
and among the Marratta tribes, as well as
in America, the fields of Indian corn are
cultivated by the women alone. The Arab
mounts his afs, and leaves his wife, with
a large bundle on her head, to follow him
on foot. The favage fits at his eafe in
his canoe, while his wife keeps tugging
at the oar without murmur or complaint.
Now it appears very remarkable that two
people inhabiting oppofite hemifpheres of
the globe, the one ancient and the other probably modern, fhould fo ftrongly refemble
each other; whilft Europeans, at an equal
diftance from both, have manners entirely
different.

In Arabia, a numerous family is an object of great defire to both fexes. Hence
an old maiden, an aged batchelor, and a
barren

barren woman, are regarded with a sentiment bordering on contempt. The husband and wife are equally delighted at the birth of a child; and upon the delivery of the first male, resign their own name, in order to take the more honourable appellation of the child's parents. Thus, should Peter and Mary have a son, James, they immediately cease to be Peter and Mary, and are styled henceforth the father and mother of James. The father of James begins to cultivate his beard, as a badge of his new-acquired dignity, as well as to attract that respect and veneration which he conceives now become due to him from the public. Of this description, among others, are the Syrian Arabs. The Arabs of the Bedouin tribes assume the name of the common stock: hence Ben Halet, or the children of Halet. A name, I conceive, by which all the individuals of the tribe are represented as brethren, is at the same time interesting to the mind, and extremely useful in society. It very sensibly implies a reciprocal obligation; in one view admonishing the children of the duty and respect they

owe

owe to their fathers; in another, engaging the parent to maintain a kind and affectionate behaviour towards children, whofe names it is his glory to bear.

From the extreme referve maintained between the fexes, we are not to expect in the circles of Syria that gaiety of manners, or highly feafoned though fuperficial converfation, to which, in different countries of Europe, a conftant and anxious defire of pleafing the women has given occafion. The youth, in the moft lively period of life, are all equally ferious in their deportment and converfation; fupporting a gravity of manners which gradually increafes as they advance in years. They fpeak but little, and never lofe fight of the object they had firft in view. A total want of vivacity, the habit of fmoking, which gives occafion to frequent paufes, and that of ftroaking their beards and handling a kind of chaplet, allow them time to confider and digeft their queftions and replies. In difcourfe they are fhort and energetic, proportioning the number of their words to the nature of the fubject in difcuffion; hence a peculiar

liar characteristic of their language, which,
if I may presume to form an opinion on
the little knowledge I was able to acquire
of it during my abode in this country, is
the most simple and expressive in the
world.

The fair sex are never introduced as a
topic of conversation; nay, they even pass
in the streets without obtaining the smallest
notice from the men. The places they are
known to frequent are deemed sacred and
inacceffible; and a man would feel himself
affronted, who should be accused of having
remarked or saluted a woman in public.
Europeans, I know, confider those eastern
manners as the gloomy result of extreme
jealousy; but I rather regard them as the
confequences of a punctilious delicacy relative to the point of honour in the sex,
who, according to the maxims of Asia, are
not suppofed to have any acquaintance
with men, except in the person of one individual. The women, neverthelefs, con-
trive to pass the time agreeably by themfelves; and as the fole object of their parties is amusement, little affected by any
ingredient

ingredient that can give occasion to latent disgust, they probably experience more real gaiety of heart than the fair European, who, in the midst of her crowded and promiscuous assemblies, is often liable to be disturbed by envy, jealousy, or resentment. With a mind easy and unembarrassed, the Asiatic seems to move in a situation which affords a finer relish for the society and enjoyment of her companions. She receives the visits of her friends in her own apartments, while the garden, the bath, and the tomb, are the places of her public resort. This Oriental custom of frequenting the tombs, is a strong proof of female sensibility; the mind being nicely susceptible of impressions, but at the same time endowed with a peculiar versatility of reflection, has stamped its own image on this kind of assembly. Upon their arrival at the grave of a deceased friend, they give full vent to the sorrow and anguish of their bosoms; afterwards they gradually enter into conversation, which takes a serious, gay, or even ludicrous turn, according to their different charac-

8

ters.

ters. After all, a good heart may here find relief; and many, I have no doubt, profit by thofe leffons of moral inftruction they receive at the grave, however extraordinary the cuftom itfelf may appear to ftrangers.

The natives of this country are extremely tenacious of ancient cuftoms; a circumftance which will account for the many veftiges we ftill trace of the manners and ufages of the ancient patriarchs. The *tanour*, or cylindrical oven, employed in baking their cakes, and the *tantoura*, or filver cone, a kind of head-drefs worn by the women among the Drufes, are evidently the fame with the Jewifh oven and Judith's mitre. The manners of Abraham and his family may be traced in the habits and purfuits of the Bedouin fhepherds, who, fince the age of Laban, have led about their flocks during the day, and folded them in the evening. The ftyle of the Arabic language in our own times is the fame with that of the Old Teftament, a famenefs which could only have been preferved by an anxious attachment to the modes and cuftoms of their progenitors.

Being originally defcended from wandering

ing tribes, they are at little pains to adorn their houfes; and the different articles of their furniture are fo contrived as to be eafily packed up for the convenience of travelling. Riding is of all exercifes that of which they are moft paffionately fond. In their perfons they are clean, fober and fimple in their manners, and entire ftrangers to luxury. The pompous and arrogant genius of the Turk has been communicated in no degree to the inhabitants of this country, whofe courage and virtuous fimplicity have hitherto bid defiance to the fetters of a defpotic mafter. They are, however, felfifh, and fometimes, though rarely, fraudulent towards the French, who, they infift, ought to pay them a certain tribute in confideration of that commerce they are permitted to carry on in their harbours. Befides, the extreme difference they difcover between the manners of France and thofe of Syria, difpofes them to look down on the natives of the former country with difdain.

In Syria we find four orders of men only: firft, princes; fecondly, lords and governors;

governors; thirdly, opulent merchants and
farmers; and laftly, the poorer peafantry,
and all below them.   A prince or lord,
provided he abftains from commerce, may
defcend from his rank in order to redeem
his decayed fortune, without lofing one
tittle of the refpect due to his birth.
The merchant and farmer, how opulent
foever their circumftances, are incapable
of rifing to a higher order, but, like the
prince, and for fimilar reafons, may defcend to a lower condition without any
diminution of his confequence; and in
many inftances the children of reduced
governors, clergymen, and merchants, are
not afhamed to enter into the fervice of
ftrangers, who are greatly their inferiors
in point of birth.   The right every individual poffeffes of redreffing his own
wrongs has given occafion to fomething
fimilar to our point of honour, which prevails equally among all orders of men.
The Arab retaliates on his adverfary,
how eminent foever his rank, the moment he receives an affront; a cuftom
which, confidering the circumftances of the
country,

country, more effectually reftrains violence than the operation of the fevereft laws for the punifhment of crimes. If the Arab fhews a conftant deference towards the perfon of his chief, it is on account of qualities really ufeful to the tribe; but as in all ranks, manners, drefs, and the fare of the table, are extremely fimilar, it is difficult on ordinary occafions to diftinguifh one order of men from another. Every one is acquainted with the high pedigree of an Arabian chieftain, who, neverthelefs, in his affability and condefcenfion to his inferiors, forms a ftriking contraft to the upftart nobility of modern nations. The prince, the lord, and the peafant, fit down to the fame table, enter familiarly into converfation, and light their pipes at the fame taper, under as little ceremony or conftraint as we expect to meet with in the fociety of brothers. In fine, men in all conditions of life eat, fleep, and work together; infomuch that I have often miftaken a lord for a peafant, and a peafant for a prince, the fuperior beauty of whofe horfe, and brightnefs of his armour, being

the

the only marks by which the latter may be known.

Wishing to become better acquainted with the natives of the Syrian mountains, I proposed to give them a little more of my time, and particularly to visit the people called Druses; meanwhile I resolved to pay my respects once more to my friends the Maronites of the Quesrouan, and accordingly my first stage was Aintoura; thence I continued my journey towards Agousta, where I hoped to have had the honour of meeting with the patriarch of Antioch. At Aintoura I saluted my friend the superior of the jesuits, who earnestly requested I would pass some time at the convent; but I excused myself, and went to sleep at Baruth.

Next day, having set out for a place named Abey, situated among the Druses, I crossed the plain of Baruth diagonally, and travelled three leagues southward. In the vicinity of the town this plain is planted with mulberries, after which I came upon a beautiful forest of pines in a quincunxial form, close to a little Arabian encampment.

campment. Paffing a dry defart foil with fome olives, and a few plantations of the mulberry, I arrived at a large village near the foot of a mountain, the refidence and patrimonial inheritance of an obfcure emir. Keeping this village on the left, I afcended by a long and fteep path, and paffed another large village on the right. Here the traveller traverfes feveral mountains, and having afcended to a confiderable height, he finds a large village named Aramon, containing a caftle or feraglio, which belongs to the family of the reigning emir. The adjacent country appears to be well watered, and is planted with olive and mulberry-trees. Having defcended from Aramon, and croffed more mountains with their intervening vallies, I at length difcovered, from the top of a high ridge, the village of Abey ftanding on an eminence before me. I paffed a little village, from whofe emir I received every attention, and arrived at Abey in the evening, after a journey of feven leagnes.

This village was once the refidence of an emir's family, which is now entirely extinct.

It

It is fituated at the diftance of two leagues
from a large town named Dair-el-Kamar,
which is the capital of the Drufean country, and the feat of the grand emir and his
relations. Its pofition, at three leagues diftance from the fea, and one from the river
Thamour, is by far the fineft I have yet
met with.   Abey is built on the third
flight of a vaft amphitheatre, formed by
three mountains piled one above another,
and occupying the whole intervening fpace
between the village and the Mediterranean.
From this lofty ridge the eye commands a
view of Sidon and Baruth, with their adjacent plains.   The defcent to the fecond
flight is formed by a fmall ridge or Afs's
Back, on each fide of which is a little
valley at the bottom of a very high and
fteep precipice : both vallies are watered
by a copious rivulet of fine water, fupplied
by the fprings in the neighbourhood of
Abey.   Thefe fprings are of great ufe
in watering the fides of the mountains,
which, notwithftanding their very abrupt
defcent, are dreffed in an amphitheatrical form, and planted with the mulberry.

VOL. II.   Q   There

There are likewife five or fix other fprings in this diftrict, on the confines of which the traveller finds fquare plantations of the walnut-tree.

I fixed my head quarters in a Capuchin convent, from the fuperior of which I met with kindnefs and hofpitality. This convent overlooks five or fix highland villages, in which I fpent the greateft part of my time; and as the great object of this excurfion was to obferve the manners of a people hitherto but little known, I omitted nothing that could introduce me to their acquaintance and good graces. Befides living with the natives, I affifted at all their ruftic diverfions, and even made myfelf ufeful to them by watching their fheep and goats; and I have the fatisfaction to think that I was the caufe of diminifhing, in fome degree, that averfion which, contrary to their own rules of hofpitality, and the regard they profefs to entertain for ftrangers, they had retained againft the French. After conforming to the life of a favage in America, a Bramin in India,

India, and an Arab in the defert, I was now
a fhepherd on the mountains of the Drufes; and often have I admired the inftincts of my goats, who, after bleating and
ftamping with their feet, as if in defiance
of the precipice that feparated them from
the flock, bound with alacrity to the
oppofite cliff. The extraordinary afpects
of the rocky ridges, which in the courfe
of my vocation I had frequently occafion
to obferve, as well as the focial and friendly intercourfe of my fellow-fhepherds, were
the grateful wages of many painful and
difficult excurfions over the diftant hills.

During my abode in this country I affifted at feveral funerals, Drufan as well as
Chriftian; ceremonies which, with a little
difference in the form of their prayers, are
in other refpects extremely fimilar. In a
few hours after he expires, the deceafed is
laid out under a tent, dreffed in his ordinary
apparel and warlike accoutrements; and
the more devout Drufes, concerning whom
I am to fpeak, place likewife a pious book
in his hands. The women haften from
all quarters, in order to feat themfelves

Q 2 around

around the corpſe, and to bedew it with their tears ; while the men, after making the vallies refound with the moſt diſmal cries and lamentations, as a ſignal to the adjacent villages of what has happened, remain in deep ſilence at a ſmall diſtance from the tent. In a little time the friends of the deceaſed are feen flocking in crowds from their reſpective villages ; and as foon as they are perceived at the tent, the neareſt relations take up the body, and ſet off to meet them. Having joined their acquaintances, they carry it at ſome diſtance from the houſes all round the village, expreſſing the moſt clamorous regret on the occaſion by cries and groans, waving their handkerchiefs in the air, and geſticulating with their bodies in a violent manner. The dead body is now returned to the tent, where the women reſume their former ſituation, repeating, however, their part of the ceremony at every new arrival of friends. Thus the body lies in a kind of ſtate till next morning, when the inhabitants of the village, Chriſtians as well as Druſes, affemble,. and having laid the

corpſe

corpfe on a bier, carry it out before the door in profound filence. Here a Catholic or Drufan prieft, according to the religion of the defunct, begins the fervice, which confifts in a number of prayers, recited in a low tone of voice. The preparations for the departure of the bier are accompanied with the moft doleful howling and even refiftance of the women, who feem unable to brook a final feparation. Meanwhile the men continue with mournful gravity to be paffive fpectators. At length the principal mourners retire weeping and inconfolable into the houfe, when it is the bufinefs of the men to conduct the deceafed to his grave. When the funeral is over the ftrangers are invited by the inhabitants of the village to their feveral houfes, where, while they commemorate the virtues of the dead, they entertain their guefts in the beft manner they are able.

I now paid a vifit to the town Dair-el-Kamar, fituated near the banks of the Thamour, and on the fide of a mountain oppofite to that on which ftands the village

of

of Abey. I paſſed the river by a bridge built in part over a cruſt of petrified clay, which preſents the traveller with rocks that had been immerſed in the mud, and tracks occaſioned by runs of water previous to the period of its petrification. El-Kamar is well ſupplied with excellent water, and ſtands at leaſt equally high with the village of Abey, but is more difficult of acceſs. The palaces or ſeraglios, which belong to the emirs of the reigning family, are fine buildings; the churches are handſome, and built in good taſte, and the houſes of ſome cheiks and commandants have large and convenient apartments, but the reſt of the town conſiſts of mean and ill-conſtructed habitations. The Druſes do not exceed one half of the inhabitants, while the remainder are all Maronites and Greek Catholics; for, owing to the zeal and induſtry of the Capuchin miſſionaries, who in the courſe of twenty years have reſtored to the communion of the Romiſh church near three-fourths of the nation, there are at preſent only a very few ſchiſmatic Greeks in thoſe parts.

The

The mountains fouth of the river Thamour are named the Land of Souf, though
Dair-el-Kamar is in this diftrict, and the
ordinary refidence of the emirs. As many
of the emirs, however, have removed to
Baruth, they are by no means fo powerful,
or of fo much confequence, here as upon
the northern parts of the river. A great
cheik in the country of Souf frequently
eludes the homage which he owes to the
authority of the grand emir. The third
and laft divifion of the mountains is inhabited by cheiks of tolerably regular and
quiet manners, as well as by two families
of emirs, who are proprietors of a very confiderable territory. The Chriftian cheiks,
or the defcendants of the houfe of Gazen,
who are the great lords of the Quefrouan,
though poffeffed of a large and populous
country, give little interruption to the
emir's government. The fact feems to
be, that the former being extremely numerous, but broken into fmall branches,
are incapable of uniting in one body, and
confequently of forming or executing any
premeditated plan of oppofition to his au-

Q 4   thority;

thority; a circumstance, the advantages accruing from which to his tranquillity have not escaped the sagacity of the grand emir, who, by sowing dissension and jealousy among their different members, is enabled to preserve the balance of power in his own hands, and to prevent their entering into any dangerous conbination against him.

The forms of legal procedure within these mountains are extremely simple. The cheik administers justice to the inhabitants of his own village; but in terminating their suits, particularly of a civil nature, he acts for the greatest part as an arbiter or umpire between the parties. If the persons concerned in the suit either decline his jurisdiction, or refuse to acquiesce in his decree, they may appeal to the court of the grand emir, who, except in actions of property situated in the Quesrouan, and holding of the house of Gazen, or belonging to inferior emirs possessing an exclusive jurisdiction over their own estates, is the ultimate and supreme judge. The administration of justice, owing to the

weak

weak ftate of civil authority, is by no means
fevere; and hence the judge feldom attempts to execute a more rigorous fen-
tence than that of quartering troops on the
delinquent, or burning his mulberry-plantations. Apprehending offenders is attended
with fuch danger and difficulty, as to render the infliction of corporal punifhment
extremely rare. A mountaineer is never
feen without the walls of his cottage un-
provided with a dagger or fabre; and if he
means to go to any confiderable diftance
from home, he is armed likewife with a
gun and piftols. By the maxims of their
confuetudinary law, a man is warranted to
repel force by force, and to redrefs his own
wrongs in the beft manner he can; and
therefore whoever conceives himfelf infulted difpatches his antagonift the moment he finds an opportunity of levelling
his piece at him, with as little concern as he
would kill a woodcock.

A man who gives his daughter in marriage to any but one of his own relations
is confidered as bringing reproach on himfelf and his tribe : and I have been told fuch

as

as have ventured to tranfgrefs this rule of family alliance have been difpatched by the dagger, before the confummation of the nuptials. Families of the fame blood entertain the moft clannifh attachment, infomuch that whoever offers an injury or affront to one, is held to be in a ftate of hoftility to the whole tribe. In a criminal accufation, befides the protection derived to the offender from the combined force of his own kindred, if he dreads an obftinate profecution on the part of the family offe ded, or at the inftance of the grand emir, and that all the power of his friends will be unable to avail him, he retires under the protection of fome cheik or inferior emir, who, in order to avoid the infamy he would incur by violating the rules of hofpitality, contributes his aid to fhelter him from the purfuit of his enemies.

Such emirs and cheiks as are not related to the reigning family, have no right to take into their fervice and pay any but the vaffals and retainers of their own eftates. But whoever is defcended
8   from

from the family of the grand emir is entitled to make his levies all over the mountains; a circumſtance which tends greatly
to cirumſcribe the emir's authority as often
as a diſpute happens between him and any
of his relations. Meanwhile it is the policy and conſtant buſineſs of the baſha to
create and foment ſuch diſſenſions, no leſs
with a view to weaken the authority of the
emir's government, than by becoming at laſt
the umpire of their quarrels, he may have
an opportunity of extorting preſents from
both parties. The interferences which
occaſionally ariſe between the emirs and
cheiks are never of equally ſerious conſequence as thoſe of individual families.
The recruits which both parties bring
into the field conſiſt of men who have
no ſtronger motive than their own caprice,
or the ties of acquaintance, to prefer the
pay of one emir or cheik to that of another.
As branches of the ſame family are ſometimes ſcattered in ſeparate villages, and
ſubject to different chiefs, it frequently happens that the father and ſon find
themſelves oppoſed to each other. The two
armies,

armies, however, thus compofed, are always fufficiently careful not to fhed the blood of their friends, out of compliment to their leaders. The chief mifchief to be apprehended in fuch fituations, is a great deal of clamour, riot, and confufion. As foon as the two armies are in prefence of each other, the cheiks and heads of the peafantry deliver their fentiments upon the matter; and as every one thinks himfelf entitled to a fhare in the adminiftration of affairs, the troops in general canvafs the grounds of the difpute in their turn. If the popular opinion happens to be in favour of a pacification, it is intimated by the cheiks to the commanders in chief, who commonly find it expedient to accede to the terms dictated by their retainers; but fhould the terms of accommodation infifted upon by the parties be fo widely different as to preclude all hopes of accommodation, the congrefs breaks up, and after committing fome devaftation on the enemy's mulberry-plantations, every man returns to his own houfe, fatisfied with what he has performed. The peafant, there-

fore,

fore, befides having had an opportunity of
difplaying his military talents, pockets the
annual pay of the emir for his fervices, and
returns to his plough, the only perfon benefited by the campaign.

But if their inteftine quarrels are tame
and inoffenfive, the wars they wage againft
ftrangers are proportionally fanguinary and
fierce ; and hence that terror with which
they are regarded by all around them. Various inftances render the fact undoubted,
that a mountaineer undertakes affaffination
at the command of the emir, and frequently
defcends alone, and in cold blood, to execute
his purpofe on the devoted victim, whether
in the city or the camp. A Drufan fome
time ago ftabbed the aga of the cuftoms at
Sidon, in the prefence of his clerks, whilft
the friend of the affaffin, a Maronite, ftood
at the gate of the town with a piftol in one
hand and a fabre in the other, in order to
cover his retreat.

The money or tribute payable to the
Grand Signior is levied by the emir from
the cheiks, who apportion it in their turn on
their refpective villages, and collect it from
individuals

individuals by a fair affeffment. But in fuch villages as hold directly of the grand emir, this tax is impofed by a rate fixed in an affembly of the inhabitants. It is competent to thofe affemblies to deliberate and decide on all bufinefs of national concern, fuch as public repairs, and the beft methods of improving and cultivating the foil. The taxes are inconfiderable, and impofed with ftrict impartiality, according to every man's property in land or cattle. The wealth of the people at large confifts chiefly in goats, which occafion no expence, and but little attention ; for fuch is the genial warmth of this climate, that at one degree of elevation in thofe regions, or another, they are affured of fine pafture at all feafons of the year,

One half of the inhabitants in the land of Souf are Chriftians ; a third are Catholic Greeks ; and the reft Maronites. The fchifmatic Greeks are fo inconfiderable in number as to be of little confequence. In the other diftricts of thofe mountains one half of the people are of the Maronitic fect, with very few either fchifmatic

or

or Catholic Greeks; the other half are compofed of Drufes, divided into two claffes: the firft have no other religion than that of nature; while the fecond, named Acquelle or fpiritual Drufes, are the followers of a religion, the principles of which are altogether unknown. The honour of belonging to this clafs is not to be attained by birth, but by a life of fimplicity, innocence, and religious penitence. Its votaries appear dreffed in black, or in a garment ftriped black and white, wear a white turban, but of a modeft form, and are not allowed, by the rules of their order, to carry arms, except when all the cheiks take the field, or in cafes of the greateft emergency. Dreading to become acceffaries to the guilt of thofe who may have acquired property by unjuft or unfair means, they never eat with, nor will receive a prefent, but from men of the moft irreproachable characters. Much of their time is fpent in reading the five books of Mofes, which in Arabic are named Taura, and at ftated times they affemble to pray in their oratories; but what thefe

oratories

oratories contain I neither had an opportunity of examining myfelf, nor of learning from others.   On the days allotted to
prayer and the fervices of the oratory, they
keep watch upon the neighbouring hills to
the diftance of half a league all around.
In houfes named *caloué*, fituated on the
tops of the moft fteep and inacceffible
rocks, and in the vicinity of their villages,
the moft devout of this order fhut themfelves up for feveral weeks together. Some,
I was affured, admit to auricular confeffion
penitents, whofe fins urge them to feek
confolation in the exercife of this Chriftian privilege.   The memory of thofe acquelle who die, as they exprefs it, in the
fweet odours of holinefs, is held in the
deepeft veneration, while their bodies have
the honour to be depofited in the little
oratory.   They practife great aufterities,
fafting, prayer, and an entire abftinence
from every fpecies of pleafure; one example I had occafion to obferve in a fpiritual at Abey, who fubfifted on bread and
water alone. In this village is the body
of an ancient Drufan, an object of great
veneration

veneration over the whole country. The acquelle enter our churches with a modeft, collected, and refpectful deportment, and in this particular fet an example to all Chriftians; though it muft be allowed that the Chriftians of thofe parts have a much more devout behaviour at divine worfhip than is always to be met with in Europe. In fine, many of the acquelle feem to attend with fatisfaction to the truths of the gofpel; but the fear of ridicule, and the forfeiture of their goods, prefent violent difficulties to their converfion. Hence the reafon why the labours of our Capu-chin miffionaries, who, by their zeal, the purity of their manners, and particu-larly their fkill in the practice of medi-cine, are highly refpected in this coun-try, have been of fo little avail. The purity and piety of their lives, however, procur-ing them accefs to the firft families, fe-veral of the emirs' wives have been con-verted to the Chriftian faith. The con-verfion of the mothers has led to the bap-tifm of fome of their children, with the confent of the emir himfelf, who from his high rank is in a condition to defpife the cenfure and reproach of his neighbours. I have fome reafon to believe there are emirs who would have little objection to be bap-tifed themfelves, provided the court of Rome, in confideration of inward confor-mity, would difpenfe with their obfervance of the external rites of the church.

The other clafs of Drufes is extremely rude and uninformed; and though fome of them are faid to worfhip the true God, they may be confidered in general as hav-ing no fixed religious opinions whatever. I am told they fometimes read the Taura, or books of Mofes ; but I can only fay, from my own obfervation, that in their perfons and deportment they are much more bar-barous and uncultivated than either the Chriftians or their more pious brethren the acquelle. Among thefe Drufes, how-ever, I have known men of very good characters. They value themfelves highly on their perfonal courage; and I am not fure that my bad opinion of their morals may not proceed from prejudice and their outward appearance.

That

That very extenfive valley ftretching in
length from Sidon to the river Ibrahim, in
breadth from the fea to Beca, and fituated
between the mountains of the Drufes and
thofe of Damafcus, properly named Anti-
Libanus, is wholly under the dominion of
the grand emir.   The tribes inhabiting the
country between Sidon and the river Thamour are brave, well made in their perfons, and confiderably civilized.   From the
Thamour all the way to the Quefrouan the
character of the people is more rude and
ferocious.   The natives of the Quefrouan
are lefs arrogant, but impatient of ftrangers, and addicted to revenge.   Laftly, in
the country above the Quefrouan, known
by the name of the Anti-Quefrouan, the
manners of the people are ftill more coarfe
and favage; and thus I was able to diftinguifh four different fhades of character
in the natives of thofe mountains.   Except, however, in certain peculiarities, the
manners of the country in general are very
much the fame.   Although a ftranger, I
lived in their villages without the leaft ap-
prehenfion either of robbery or affaffina-

tion;

tion; and, during the three months I paffed at Abey, flept in a garden near the
great road, without wall or fence of any
kind, and without meeting with the fmalleft
difturbance.

I had easy accefs to the fociety of twelve
villages in the neighbourhood. Near that
of Roche-maya I was fhewn the enormous
fragment of a mountain, which, undermined in procefs of time, had rolled down
into a valley watered by the Thamour. A
village and feveral little hamlets lay buried
under the ruins, and the courfe of the
current was for fome time completely interrupted; but the river gradually wafhing
away the loofe and earthy parts of the
mafs, at length recovered its ufual channel.

I now quitted my abode in this part of
the country, in order to make a fecond
vifit to Mafra-Cafan de Bian, which, as I
had occafion to mention in my firft expedition, is fituated at the foot of the
higheft mountain in the Quefrouan; I
therefore proceeded to Baruth, and after
vifiting my acquaintance at Aintoura and
Jelton, foon joined my good friend the
paftor

paſtor of Mafra, where, though in the end of June, I found the houſes ſtill occupied by the ſilk-worm, which ſupplies the general and moſt lucrative objcct of induſtry in thoſe regions.

I likewiſe viſited a village named Beca Touta, whoſe cheik the preceding year conducted me to view the inſcription of Elfogra : he was very happy to ſee me, and under his protection I went to viſit a handſome female convent of Greek Catholics. This building was erected by a rich merchant of Damaſcus, who after ſmarting long under the yoke of Turkiſh ſervitude, had retired to paſs the evening of his life in the quiet of thoſe mountains. I ſaw alſo, in a ſequeſtered corner of the ſame diſtrict, the eſtates of the Beſconta emirs, who are eſteemed men of great power and conſequence.

Having now made a conſiderable ſtay in this part of Aſia, and being inclined to paſs into Europe without loſs of time, I proceded directly to St. Jean d'Acre, a port much frequented by the trading ſhips of Marſeilles.

At

At Baruth, Sidon, and ftill more at this place, I made acquaintance with families of Greek origin, whofe manners are by no means equally pure with thofe of the Arabs, and whofe minds, formed to all that delicacy, art, and fubtlety difcoverable in the refinement of their language, are far from being agreeable to my fentiments. In exchange for the honeft heart, manly good fenfe, and naïve vivacity of the Arab, though at times a little ferocious in his temper, I could find nothing in them but the ftudied levity of a deceitful and inte-refted mind. This reflection led me to make a brief comparifon of the different races of fimple men I had had an opportunity of feeing in the courfe of my travels; and having confidered them in their manners, the entire freedom of their fituation, and their peculiar vigour both of mind and body, I am obliged to hefitate between the Arab and American favage: perhaps, however, the principles of action in the former ought to throw the fcale in his favour, in preference to any other defcrip-tion of men whatever. The pleafant and

dexterous

dexterous genius of the Biſſayan Indians, the ſuavity of manners inherent in the natives of India, and that goodneſs of heart in common to all thoſe ſimple people, united to the ſuperior excellency of their climate and ſoil, give them many advantages in my mind over the condition of Europeans, whether conſidered as to their country, climate, or manners.

C H A P. VI.

A Voyage from St. Jean d'Acre. to the Port of Marſeilles, touching at the Iſland of Rhodes, Malta, Tunis, and Sardinia.

SETTING ſail for Marſeilles in the end of June 1771, we bore away for the iſland of Cyprus; and having coaſted it with a weſterly, and conſequently a contrary wind, prevalent in thoſe parts during the ſummer months, we ſtretched northward in order to catch the breeze from that quarter, and accordingly found it on the coaſt of Caramania. It is obſervable that I had experienced a weſt

R 4   wind

wind ever fince my departure from Surat;
a wind which blows generally, during the
fummer feafon, from the line all the way
to the ifland of Candia; generally I fay,
for we muft except certain intervals, in
which the land breeze prevails. As foon
as we came upon the coaft in the gulph
of *Satalia*, we faw a fmall veffel, which
getting into our wake bore down upon us
with full fail. Apprehenfive fhe might prove
one of thofe piratical cruizers, which the
Ruffian and French armed fhips had driven from the Archipelago into thofe parts,
though we obferved only one man on
board, who was at the helm, we fired a
fhot; but fhe perfifted in her courfe, and it
was not till we had repeated our falute
that fhe at laft chofe to fheer off.

As we approached the fouthern coaft
of the ifland Rhodes, finding we were in
want of water, we touched at an out-
port named Limba from an adjacent village. About half way from the top of
a mountain in its vicinity ftand the ruins
of two forts, which were anciently built
by the knights of Rhodes. We were
supplied

supplied with water and fresh provisions
from the Grecian villages; but I could
not help constantly comparing the refined
Greek with the hardy Arabian; the Greek's
cruel servitude under the Turk, with that
high-spirited freedom and independence
which cleave to the rustic but manly life
of the Arab; the polished address, nice food,
smart apparel, and neat apartments of the
former, with the coarse and rude state of all
those articles that fall to the share of the
latter; and was upon the whole confirmed,
that in all societies of men extreme civili-
zation and refinement are certain presages
of approaching decline. I observed with
sincere concern how widely those two
races of men differ from each other in their
notions of happiness, the object of their
joint pursuit. The Greek is gay, but
selfish; poor, and yet delicate in every
thing that relates to the gratification of
his appetites. The Arab is lively and ge-
nerous, equally poor with the Greek;
but has few wants that can occasion
him a moment's pain or inquietude. What
an extreme difference between those two
people!

people ! and how ill conſtituted the one to attain real happineſs, compared with the other ! The moſt miſerable of the two, however, paſſes his days amidſt all the advantages of an indulgent ſky; whilſt the other roams the naked face of a deſert, which in many reſpects is unpropitious to the contented enjoyment of life.

Perceiving ſymptoms of ſuſpicion in the Turks that we had come hither in order to procure proviſions for the Ruſſian ſhips, we made haſte to get again under weigh; and, indeed, we had no ſooner got clear of the bay, than we obſerved a veſſel near the ſhore, ſtealing towards us with little ſail. She preſently diſcovered by our motions that ſhe had not eſcaped our obſervation, and therefore, ſetting all her canvaſs, inſtantly gave us chace. As we would not betray our apprehenſions of danger, we hoiſted our flag and pendant; but the enemy, which proved to be a chebec with Turkiſh colours, probably miſtaking us for a ſhip of war, when ſhe came a little nearer ſuddenly bore away, a circumſtance which gave us no ſmall ſatisfaction :

for,

for, had we been vifited, as a part of our
cargo confifted of rice, contrary to an or-
dinance of the Porte, we muft have been
carried back to the ifland of Rhodes, where
it is difficult to fay how long we might
have been detained.

I was extremely forry to obferve the very
little regard entertained by the Turks for
Europeans in general, and particularly for
the French. The confideration of what
might have been the iffue of our being
attacked and captured by this chebec naturally led me to thefe reflections; and I
began to bring under review what I had
learned from others, as well as what I had
obferved myfelf, refpecting our commerce
and factories in Syria, and other parts of
the Levant; and I am perfuaded, that befides the difference of religion and manners
fubfifting between us and the Afiatics,
which neceffarily gives occafion to a mutual eftrangement, the conduct of the
French in thofe countries contributes ftill
more to annihilate our confequence in the
eftimation of the Turks.

I obferved that our merchants in the
fea-ports

fea-ports of the Levant are often obliged
to precipitate their commercial tranfactions
in order to fatisfy the demands of their
European correfpondents;—that they conduct themfelves with little method or fteadinefs in their engagements with the natives, whofe uniform accuracy in bufinefs
forms a ftriking contraft with the giddi-
nefs and levity of the European merchant;
—that the Turkifh governors, from an extreme intimacy which fubfifts between
them and the merchants, are too much
acquainted with their commercial as well
as private affairs, and hence have it in
their power to thwart fuch fchemes and
fpeculations of the conful and company
as may not coincide with their own views;
—that certain favoured houfes, named *bara-
taires*, make themfelves fubfervient to the
finifter policy of the bafha refpecting mo-
nopolies, practices to which he finds himfelf invited by the meannefs and fervility
of the merchants, while he is thereby em-
boldened to refufe their reafonable requefts
as often as he may find it expedient. I
will not fay it muft be always improper

in

in the merchant to make prefents to the
governor, or even to affift him with money in cafes of great emergency; but I
maintain, that the merchant ought to poffefs fuch a degree of fpirit and independence as might enable him to refift thofe
loans, which are equivalent to extortion,
and have no other object than the gratification of official avarice. Good offices,
feafonably and frankly beftowed, are no lefs
formed to engage the gratitude and efteem
of a high-minded people like the Turks,
than fervices, originating in fear, and
performed in a fneaking and defpicable
manner, are fitted to excite their contempt.

The French have a certain number of
fhips conftantly employed in the Levant,
as carriers for the Turkifh merchants.
Now I am extremely doubtful whether
the profits returned by this branch of
traffic into the national coffers can be
faid to be an equivalent for the defertion
of our feamen, the corruption of their
manners, and that lofs of reputation which,
by becoming the hirelings of ftrangers, we
fuftain

sustain as a kingdom, in the estimation of the Turks themselves. Whatever might be the sentiments of a Dutchman or Rugusan upon a point in which interest and honour are so much involved, I am confident no Englishman or Spaniard would be inclined to follow our example.

The European consul in the Levant seldom transacts business with the governor but by the mouth of his dragoman, who has often little acquaintance with the language of the country, and is always basely subservient to the will of the basha and his subordinate officers. Hence the requisitions of the consul have little weight; and unless methods more persuasive than the mediation of the dragoman can be devised, have little chance of being complied with. If an affair of some delicacy and importance comes to be negociated through the medium of the dragoman, an arrogant basha, forgetting the respect due to a great nation, is apt to treat the French, in the person of so humble a representative, with insolence and indignity; whereas a man invested with the commission, and a cer-

tain

tain part of the fovereign's delegated authority, is a character of a more impofing
nature, and would accordingly obtain much
more confideration.

We continued our voyage by the canal
of Candia; and afterwards, directing our
courfe for the coaft of Malta, on the 15th
of October we came to anchor at that
ifland. Here I met with feveral French
frigates, on board of which were fome of
my old companions, whofe friendfhip for
me was not impaired by my long abfence.

We again put to fea, and after a navigation of fix days the fhip's owner having
bufinefs at Tunis, we ftood for that port,
where I was kindly received by the French
conful. By his means I became acquainted with feveral Mahometans, whofe difpofitions feemed more analogous to the
amiable qualities of the Bedouin Arabs of
Baffora and Mafcate, than to the harfh
and imperious manners of the Syrian Muffulmen. We got again under fail; but
being much retarded by contrary winds,
it was not till the 27th of November that

† we

we reached the coaſt of Sardinia, where we put in, and remained two days in the gulph of Palma.   In this place, ſo near to my native country, I diſcerned with ſincere pleaſure ſome remains of man's natural ſimplicity, which revived all my regret for the honeſt and undepraved manners of our anceſtors.

The firſt perſon that ſtruck my notice on ſhore, was a man with a long beard, brawny and vigorous, who in thick and ſubſtantial clothing attended a large herd of cattle, as they grazed a piece of marſhy ground on the borders of the road.   He was mounted on a beautiful horſe, with a gun ſlung acroſs his ſhoulders.   His dwelling was among the neighbouring mountains, where, a ſtranger to refined and degenerate manners, he adheres to the ancient and ſimple uſages of his fathers; and where his own courage and independence of mind have hitherto in ſome meaſure ſet the arms of the conqueror at defiance. The neatneſs and ſimplicity of his dreſs, the firm and manly expreſſion of his eye, and the excellent condition of his flocks,

as

as well as the dexterity he difplayed in the management of his horfe and gun, were in my mind fo many powerful arguments for his continuing to defpife the a ˙Gcial education of the citizen, and to che.˙ifh the ruftic and fimple manners of his native hills.

Having again put to fea, we left the coaft of Sardinia to the weft; paffed at fome diftance from the ifland of Corfica; and after a paffage of feven days, entering the gulph of Marfeilles, we landed on the ifle Pomeques, a place deftined for the quarantine of all fuch veffels as arrive from the ports of the Levant. Next day, being the 5th of December 1771, I entered the infirmary of Marfeilles, in order to perform quarantine ;—and gave thanks to God, for having conducted me in fafety to the end of my travels.

F I N I S.

4. The History of Manchester, with plates, 2 vols. 4to. by the fame author, 1 l. 16 s. boards.—Thefe volumes contain the Roman, the Roman-Britifh, and the Saxon periods of our hiftory.

5. Letters chiefly from India, containing an account of the military tranfactions on the coaft of Malabar during the late war; together with a fhort defcription of the religion, manners, and cuftoms of the inhabitants of Indoftan; by John le Couteur, Efq; captain in his Majefty's hundredth regiment of foot. Tranflated from the French. 8vo. 6 s. in boards.

The fame book, in French, 4 s. fewed.

6. Orations of Lyfias and Ifocrates, tranflated from the Greek, with fome account of their lives, and a difcourfe on the hiftory, manners, and character of the Greeks, from the conclufion of the Peloponnefian war to the battle of Chæronea. By John Gillies, LL. D. 4to. 1 l. 1 s. in boards.

7. Stuart's Hiftory of the Reformation of Religion in Scotland, 4to. 10 s. 6 d. in boards.

8. A View of Society in Europe, in its Progreffion from Rudenefs to Refinement; or, enquiries concerning the hiftory of law, government, and manners, 4to. 15 s. in boards. By the fame author.

9. An Hiftorical Differtation concerning the Antiquity of the Englifh Conftitution. 8vo. fecond edition, 5 s. bound. By the fame.

10. Annals of Scotland, from the Acceffion of Robert I. furnamed Bruce, to the Acceffion of the Houfe of Stewart. By Sir David Dalrymple, Bart. one of the Judges of the Court of Seffion in Scotland. 2 vols. 4to. 1 l. 7 s. 6 d. in boards.

11. An Hiftorical View of the Englifh Government, from the Settlement of the Saxons in Britain to the Acceffion of the Houfe of Stewart. By John Millar, Efq; 4to. 18 s. in boards.

12 Millar's Origin of the Diftinction of Ranks; or, an enquiry into the circumftances which gave rife to influence

influence and authority in the different members of fociety. 8vo. 6 s.

13. Campbell's Lives of the Britifh Admirals, with maps and cuts, brought down to 1779. 4 vols. large 8vo. 1 l. 8 s.-bound.

14. Dr. Macfarlan's Tracts on Subjects of National Importance: 1. on the advantages of manufactures, commerce, and great towns, to the population or profperity of a country; 2. difficulties ftated to a propofed affeffment of the land tax, and another fubject of taxation propofed not liable to the fame objection. 8vo. 1 s. 6 d.

15. Lord Lyttelton's Dialogues of the Dead. 8vo. 5 s.

16. Captain Inglefield's Narrative, concerning the lofs of his Majefty's fhip the Centaur, of 74 guns, and the miraculous prefervation of the pinnace, with the captain, mafter, and ten of the crew, in a traverfe of near 300 leagues on the great weftern ocean, with the names of the people faved, and of the officers left in the fhip, and fuppofed to have perifhed. Alfo, to this edition is annexed the proceedings of the court-martial on Captain Inglefield, for the lofs of the faid fhip. 8vo. 1 s.